*"My soul has deserted this ship
and my heart has frozen over.
Everything that made me human is now gone.
I am a monster.
This monster they've turned me into.
Out of all of them, Fox is the one
I despise the most.
He's a fool if he thinks I won't make him pay
the price for his sins.
He's a fool if he believes I will ever forget."*

- Stephen Richards

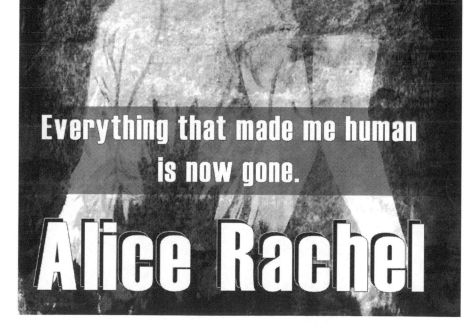

Holding Ground

A Stephen Richards
Novella 2

Everything that made me human
is now gone.

Alice Rachel

Ma chérie,

Par toi, mon coeur autrefois adouci

Par eux, est aujourd'hui anéanti.

Stephen

UNDER GROUND SERIES

Recommended Reading Order

LIST OF CHARACTERS

This list contains **SPOILERS** of *Under Ground* and *Standing Ground*—the first books in the series. Do not read this list if you haven't read the previous books.

Holding Ground starts where *Losing Ground* left off, right when Stephen and his parents are taken to Camp 19.

The series should be read in a specific order so as to avoid any confusion or spoilers.

Order of the novels and short stories:

CHARACTERS:

Stephen Richards - Chi's twin brother - Middle class.

Willow Jenison - Stephen's love interest - Middle class - Unwanted born illegally.

Chi Richards (pronounced "shy") - Stephen's twin brother - Middle class - Unwanted born illegally - Underground rebel.

Thia Clay - (pronounced "thy-ee-ah") - Upper class - Chi's love interest.

William Fox - Thia's promised fiancé in *Under Ground* - Upper class elite member - Was killed by Stephen in *Under Ground*.

Dimitri Fox - William's father - Main share-holder of the corporation training all the guards and officers in New York State - Head supervisor of said guards and officers - Upper class elite member.

Tina Davis - Chief civil officer - Upper class elite member - Underground rebel - In *Under Ground*, Tina betrayed Chi and revealed his location at Oliver's house, which led to Chi's arrest and Oliver's execution - In *Standing Ground*, it was implied that Tina may have been framed by her coworker Bryan Harris.

Bryan Harris - State officer - Underground rebel - Informant for Taylor Jones in the Underground - In *Under Ground*, Harris helped Chi escape custody after his arrest - He also told William where to find the rebels at the end of

Under Ground, inadvertently leading William to his death - Read *William's Short Story* for more information on Bryan Harris.

Neil Wilcox - Husband of Jane Wilcox - Neil sheltered Chi when Chi's parents were taken to Camp 19 two years before *Under Ground*.

Jane Wilcox - Wife of Neil Wilcox - Adopted Chi as her own child the moment he appeared on her threshold after his parents were taken away.

Jake Smith - Camp officer - Part of Shawn's team in the Underground - In *Standing Ground*, Jake and Tina broke Chi and Thia out of jail and it was revealed that Jake is in fact a double-agent working for Dimitri Fox.

James Malone - Truck driver taking food from Camp 19 to the slums of New York City - Underground rebel - Was killed by Stephen In *Under Ground* - Read *Akio's Short Story* for more information about James.

Aline Richards - Chi and Stephen's mother - Died of pneumonia In Camp 19.

Jack Richards Chi and Stephen's father - Was killed by Stephen in *Under Ground*.

Joy - William's lover in *William's Short Story*.

OFFICERS' RANKS:

1 - **Chief civil officers** - Highest ranked officers in New York State. They supervise the state officers in their divisions.

2 - **State officers** - Officers of various ranks and duties in New York State. Some state officers work as double agents under the supervision of Dimitri Fox.

3 - **Camp officers** - Officers supervising the camp guards.

4 - **Camp guards** - Guards in charge of the surveillance of the camps.

5 - **Truck drivers** - Low-rank officers driving food from the camps to the lower class members of New York State.

6 - **Trainees** - Males training to become officers or guards.

Prologue

Daddy is standing right in front of me with his belt in his hands. I know what's coming. He won't beat me up with it. He doesn't need to. I can't move. I'm too scared.

I tried. I tried so hard. When we were having dinner tonight, I didn't look at him. I thought maybe if I ignored him, he'd forget about me.

I can't breathe. I know what he has planned for me. He comes to my room almost every night.

I'm frozen in fear.

He takes one step forward, but I can't run. I'm pressed hard against the wall.

Please, let it swallow me whole.

Please, let me disappear.

I close my eyes.

Disappear.

Disappear.

Disappear.

Let me disappear.

I open my eyes.

Daddy is still here. He's closer now.

He smiles at me and I shudder.

There's nowhere safe for me to hide.

Nowhere safe for me to run.

I swallow a cry. I swallow a whimper. I blink to push away the tears. Tears are useless. They never stop Daddy anyway.

I'm frozen.

And Daddy is still smiling.

"Be a good boy now, Stephen."

He's hovering over me. He's so tall.

I'm breathing so fast that my chest hurts. I scan the room for a way out.

Out.

I need out.

"You know Daddy loves you, don't you, Stephen? Now come over here, my sweet boy."

Daddy sits on the bed and instead of running away, I do as he says. I'm so scared of disappointing him.

Daddy said that if I didn't show him love, he would abandon me and the officers would come pick me up. "Because," he said, "the officers always come for mean, ungrateful little boys."

I'm scared Daddy might call them. I'm scared Daddy might stop loving me and then his eyes will fill with hatred like Mommy's. I don't want Daddy to hate me like Mommy does. I don't know what I did to make Mommy hate me. But I must have done something wrong because Mommy still seems to love Chi very much. So why does she hate me?

Daddy said the officers would come for me. He said they'd come for Chi too and it'd be my fault.

I'm more scared of them than I am scared of him.

I don't want the officers to take my brother away.

I don't want Chi to hurt, so I let Daddy hurt me instead.

Daddy looks me in the eyes. I'm frozen on the spot. I beg him not to touch me, please, because I don't like it, but he smiles. And I'm so scared.

I start crying, but he doesn't seem to notice.

I don't move.

Each night, small pieces of me die.

One by one.

Every night.

And hatred slowly fills my heart.

And my head.

I fill my head with images instead.

Anything.

Anything.

Anything I can think of.

I'm not here.

I'm flying. I'm flying to a faraway place.

But the hatred grows.

It never goes away.

I don't think it's normal to hate Daddy like I do.

I want Daddy to love me. But the way he loves me hurts. I want Daddy to love me the same way he loves Chi. I know he doesn't touch Chi.

Why does Daddy touch me and not Chi?

Daddy whispers things in my ear that I don't want to hear. I sing, sing loud inside my head, but his words still come through. His words make me feel dirty, nasty.

I don't like it.

I don't like it.

I want him to stop.

Make him stop!

Please, someone, make him stop!

Tears run down my cheeks and I holler in my pillow, but no one ever comes to save me. I beg him not to touch me anymore. I beg him to stop.

The pillow swallows my tears. The pillow swallows my cries. But the pillow never swallows my pain.

Someone, anyone, please help me!

20

Chapter 1

Stephen - Seventeen Years Old

I come to and open my eyes to sharp pains stabbing inside my skull and at my shoulder.

Where's Willow?

I sit up straight. I'm in a room with white walls, both foreign and cold. A man dressed in black is standing by the entrance, and when he notices that I'm no longer unconscious, he grabs a phone by the door and dials one single digit.

"He's awake, Sir."

I don't know where I am. I don't know how I got here.

She went for him. Mother went for Chi, but she let them take you away.

Because you are nothing.

I tell the voices to shut the hell up, but they keep on taunting me.

You are worthless, worthless, worthless.

My wrists are tied to the arms of a chair and my ankles to its feet. I've been stripped of my clothes. I'm only wearing my old gray boxer briefs. *What is this place?*

I close my eyes. My head aches with sledgehammers pounding and pounding. I focus and try to understand what the hell I'm doing here.

The officers came to our house last night and grabbed me. Mother went to protect Chi, but she left me in the middle of the living room. I was too stunned to run and hide.

And now, I don't know where I am.

There's blood on my chest.

I look down.

The blood is like a crimson river that flowed its way down my abs.

It's dry.

The blood is mine.

I was shot.

The wound at my shoulder has been treated already. A rudimentary bandage is wrapped around it. But the pain is still there, throbbing.

The door opens and a tall, bulky blond man walks in. He's not dressed like the officer. Instead, he's wearing a dark navy blue suit tailored to his size. He reeks of money, power, and something else that sends a chill of terror down my spine. But I sit up, with my back straight, and behold him with feigned confidence.

He stands over me while holding his hands behind his back. He's probably trying to impress me and make me recoil. I hold my chin high.

"Mr. Richards." His voice is cold—freezing really.

He knows who I am.

He knows my name. My real name. Not the fake one I always use for school.

How does he know my name?

"I'm delighted to finally meet you."

The feeling isn't mutual.

"Your parents tried to go back on our little arrangement, but I finally found you."

I have no idea what he's talking about. *What arrangement?*

"But I'm still missing one out of this pair. You see, the agreement was for me to get the two of you." He sighs heavily. "I'm highly disappointed in your parents. But surely you can help me with this predicament."

He towers over me with his eyes pinning me down, and I still don't understand what the hell he's talking about.

"Surely you know where your brother is."

Ah, that's what this is about. He wants Chi.

The man points at a table close by. "See, I do not wish to use these on you. If you reveal your brother's location, this will go faster and we can finally get started with your training."

I send him a skeptical glance and look at the table. The implements lying on top shoot a tremor through my back. Scissors, knives, scalpels, and instruments of all kinds are exposed like a morbid display on a white clinical cloth. This is what he has reserved for me.

I've heard the rumors. I know what happens to the rebels. I know what the officers do to them. And that's what's coming my way. And yet I feel strangely at peace. Maybe Death has heard my request at last and this will finally be it for me. I do not care for life as much as this man thinks. Death is something I've been longing for. For a *very* long time.

The man leans toward me, with his face only inches from mine, and his breath invades my nose with hints of peppermint and smoke.

"Oh, trust me, we won't make it quick," he snickers. "Speak and you will be free rapidly. Refuse to cooperate and this is will be long and painful." He turns around while talking. "Now, where was I?" He pauses dramatically. "Ah yes, where is your brother, Mr. Richards? Chi can't have gone very far now, can he?"

How does he know Chi's name? This man knows more about us than I'm comfortable with.

Whatever he has reserved for me, I will take it.

He sends me a glance and when I don't respond, he beckons his officer to join us. The officer grabs something from the table and holds it in such a way that I can't see what it is. Nothing good, I presume.

I roll my eyes and that jerk smiles at me sadistically when he finally shows me the butcher knife he was hiding behind his back. Small shivers ripple through my skin. I wriggle in my seat and the blond man laughs.

24

With his hand on my chest, the officer pushes me back against the seat.

He shoots me a look that makes my flesh rise in goose bumps, and the cutting begins. With small incisions through my skin. On my arms and my legs at first. I clench my jaw and try hard not to groan under the pain.

When I don't give in, the cuts grow deeper, turning into vicious slashes. First on my upper arms. Then on my chest.

I clench my fists under the sharp, agonizing sensations.

The blade slices and I wince every time.

The blond man's eyes sparkle with amusement as blood comes seeping out of my wounds in tiny droplets dripping to the ground. The blade slits deeper through my chest in long linear cuts. And then my abs. And finally my shoulders.

I grit my teeth.

My breathing quickens.

I'm almost hyperventilating.

My vision blurs for a second.

But not a single sound comes out.

The blond man in navy blue is disappointed. Fox, he said his name is.

Fox is disappointed.

He tells me to call him "Sir." He can go to hell. I have no respect for these people.

Fox looks at the officer. "Let's introduce our friend Stephen to the cat."

My heart races. I try to calm down.

To no avail.

I've read about the cat of nine tails.

This torture is gonna rise to a whole new scale.

The officer picks up the whip from the table. And I try not to panic.

Fox comes to stand in front of me, with a grin plastered on his stupid face. He and his brainless acolyte untie the leather holding my wrists. They force me off the chair and I want to fight them, but their hands tighten around my upper arms as they drag me to a wooden beam and pull my wrists high above my head. Within seconds, I'm locked in place, though I wriggle to try and pull free.

I won't stop moving. The officer grabs my left leg to force it into shackles. But I knee him hard in the chin. He lets out a growl, his eyes turning murderous as he grabs my ankle and coerces me to comply. When he goes for my other leg, I try to kick him in the face, but he's too fast. Too quickly, both my feet are tied to the ground. I can't pull free.

I glare at Fox. When I'm out of the chains, I'm gonna kill the bastard.

"Tsk, tsk, Stephen," Fox says with a smirk, "just tell me where your twin is hiding and we won't need to go through with this."

I look straight at him and spit in his face. He will never find Chi.

Fox sighs and shakes his head. Then he nods at the officer who's standing behind me.

26

And then the whip falls, lacerating my skin.

And each time the lashes hit and score, tears roll down my cheeks against my will.

I grit my teeth and swallow the sounds rising in my throat.

But the lashes rip and rip and rip through my skin.

I don't give in, but I can no longer contain the screams escaping my mouth.

My skin bursts open. My vision blurs.

Everything stings.

Everything burns.

Everything hurts.

I won't make it. I won't survive this.

I grit my teeth and say nothing.

Fox is furious. He's not getting the results he wanted. I'm not caving in the way he expected me to. He tells me there's more coming my way, but I can hardly hear him. My ears are buzzing. I lost a lot of blood when I was shot last night. I'm dizzy already.

I waver.

My flesh rips under the whip.

In long slashes down my back.

Oozing blood.

More blood.

So much blood.

Whoosh. The sound of the whip slits through the air. Followed by a burning sensation. And a scream from my mouth. The room spins in front of my eyes.

27

Agony.

The voices start screaming. The voices want me dead.

You're pathetic, pathetic, pathetic.

But Death isn't coming.

I'm begging, pleading Death to free me.

Fox groans with rage. He calls two guards and the two morons take me out of my shackles and haul me toward the infirmary. They pull me by my armpits, my legs dragging on the floor as they lug me through the halls.

I'm too beat to stand up.

I'm too beat to fight back.

My ears whistle. My ears hum.

My vision blurs.

I can't see.

Anything.

I faint into darkness.

***

I come to, lying face-down on a cot. A woman wearing scrubs walks over and starts rubbing some antibiotic cream all over my back. The cold lotion burns and I flinch every time she touches the slashes with it.

She tells me to sit up. Then she takes off the bandages from around my shoulder. When she sees the bullet wound, she mumbles to herself, "Idiots. They didn't disinfect it correctly. It's oozing puss."

She gives me a look. "I'm gonna have to fix it, or it won't heal right. Sorry, handsome, it will hurt. Here, take a good bite."

She places a cloth between my teeth.

"Ready?"

Not really, but what am I supposed to say? Apparently, those people have never heard of anesthesia. Probably too humane.

She doesn't look at me once as she cuts off the stitches and disinfects the wound. My jaw tightens in spite of me.

"The bullet is lodged in too deep to take out," she says, with a casual shrug while I snarl against the cloth.

And then she sews the wound closed, one stitch at a time, the needle plunging into my skin and coming back out, and then back in again and back out.

Shit, this fucking hurts, damn it!

I grit my teeth, wince, curse, and groan into the cloth clutched in my mouth.

The nurse hums while taking care of me. She must love torturing people with peroxide, antibiotic creams, needles, and all that. This place is filled with lunatics, apparently.

"You'll come back to me tomorrow so I can change the dressing."

I don't tell her Fox has promised me more fun tomorrow as well.

In fact, he told me he was going to play with me until I tell him where Chi is. So I've got lots of fun coming because there's no way I'm telling that asshole where to find my brother.

When the nurse is done, she pats me on the cheek. "See you tomorrow, handsome boy."

She winks at me and I wrinkle my nose. I hate this place. *Seriously, what's wrong with these people?*

The guards grasp my arms and drag me through the halls, all the way to a filthy cell. Then they force me out of my blood-stained clothes and into some marine blue outfit too big for my skinny frame.

I'm too tired to fight back.

They throw me on a concrete bed covered with a thin mattress and no pillow.

"See you tomorrow, Richards," one of them says with a wicked smile on his face.

I want to flip him off, but I'm too wiped out to react or sit up. The pain is still throbbing through my flesh, blurring my sight, exhausting me.

I pass out.

Chapter 2

The next morning, two guards come to force me out. Fox has more misery reserved for me, I guess. Whatever it is, I will take it.

The men drag me to a different room this time.

They open the door and I squint my eyes, blinded by a light so bright I can't see.

My pupils adjust eventually and I make them out.

Two shapes.

Indistinct at first.

And then clear.

Too clear.

Mother and Father.

They are tied to two different chairs, and they're wearing the same kind of prisoner's garment I was forced into last night.

My parents raise their heads, and Mother runs her eyes all over my body. I'm wearing nothing but pants. The guards stripped me on purpose. I'm topless, exposed for my parents to see. Fox probably wants to draw pity out of them. This shows how little that man knows about my family. About our relationship.

I hold Mother's gaze, challenging her to feel something, anything. She has the decency to gasp when she realizes what they've done to me. But her shock doesn't last long and her face turns cold quickly.

She looks me straight in the eye one last time. One simple glance to tell me she won't save me. And that whatever they have planned for me, she will let it happen.

Father barely even reacts to my appearance. His eyes are wide open as if this is some nightmare he might still wake up from.

But this isn't a nightmare.

This is real.

I know it all too well.

The guard pushes me in the back and forces me to walk. I stand tall though my flesh hurts and my muscles ache. I stride with dignity toward a large leather chair.

I won't show my parents what this is doing to me.

I don't even glimpse their way.

This isn't about them.

This is about me.

This is about me trying to hold on, for Chi.

I will not tell these people where my brother is.

The guard forces me to sit down. He replaces my cuffs with leather ties attached to the armrests. And when my back hits the seat, I wince.

Fox comes in just then—a dramatic entrance meant to astound us. He looks ridiculous, but I can't find it in me to laugh. If this is anything like yesterday, it promises to be painful.

Fox walks to my parents and takes a seat facing them. He tells the guards to leave, but the officer by the door is asked to stay. Fox doesn't introduce himself to my parents. He calls them by their first names as if they are old acquaintances meeting at some friendly school reunion.

"Jack. Aline." He nods a greeting, but my parents don't respond.

Fox strokes his chin and sighs heavily. *What a grotesque actor playing an absurd pantomime!*

"You really let me down," he says with a shake of his head. "I thought we had an agreement. I was to have both boys when they reached the age of nine. But then you disappeared. You can only imagine my disappointment."

He turns his large, muscular frame toward me. "So now I have this one." He flicks his hand my way. "But I'm still missing the other boy."

He clears his throat. "I tried to pull some information out of Stephen, but he's more stubborn than I gave him credit for. I wish it didn't have to come to this, but you leave me no other choice. You can either reveal Chi's location to me now, or I can draw it out of your other son. And he *will* cave eventually. You might as well spare him the pain."

His eyes pin on my parents. "I believe you know the meaning of the chair he's sitting on. I'm sure this isn't something you wish upon your own child."

An irresistible need to laugh overtakes me. I chuckle once, then louder and louder until it sounds like thunder rolling out of my throat. This man is such an idiot. I laugh in my seat, and my parents stare at me like I've lost my mind.

Fox cuts me a sharp glance. "And what, exactly, do you find so funny, Stephen?"

I look at my parents before shooting Fox a disdainful smirk.

He won't get anything out of them.

Whatever he has planned for me, it won't work on my parents. I don't matter to them. I never have. And I never will.

Fox has caught the wrong son.

The one who's disposable.

Fox is waiting for me to answer or for my parents to react. He's waiting for something, frozen in a theatrical pause fitting so well with his charade. When he doesn't get what he was expecting, he sighs deeply and shakes his head. The game hasn't even started yet, but we're already proving to be awful players.

He stands up, and I wriggle in my seat to try and pull free.

Fox walks over and shows me two electrodes while grinning in my face. He says to my parents, "Of course, the chair is only here for visual effects. It's incredible how people still fear the mere sight of it. You would think that after all this time our citizens would have forgotten the meaning of the chair, but I guess horror holds a strong grip on our minds. As you know, we had to change the device. Dead prisoners are no use to me. This will barely feel worse than a stun gun. I mean..." He laughs to himself as he attaches an electrode to my calf and the other one to my lower arm. "Of course, it will hurt. What's the point otherwise, right? But the amperage isn't strong enough to kill Stephen." He taps me on the cheek a couple of times and I jerk my face away. "It will just hurt really, really badly."

He shoots a cold smile at my parents while forcing my skull back against the headrest. I try to move out of the way, but he grabs my cheeks between his fingers.

"Tsk, tsk. Now, now, Stephen, be a good boy."

He locks my head in place with a leather band wrapped around my forehead. I can't move.

Fox signals to his officer standing by the door, and the man lifts a switch. Electricity hits my body, hard. I convulse and my back arches while my hands twitch. A deep wail escapes my throat, drawn out by surprise and agony.

My heart will stop. This time, I won't make it.

I'm ready to welcome death, but the current stops just in time for my heart to resume its useless beat. My body sags with relief. My muscles spasm out of my control. And my soul deflates. The bastard didn't lie. It hurts like hell. But it won't kill me.

The officer lifts the switch again, and my teeth clamp together so hard they might break.

Every time, Fox asks my parents the exact same question he did before. He demands to know Chi's location.

And every time, my parents' eyes shift toward me, then back to Fox.

Not once do they reply.

The officer lifts the switch again, but not a single word passes my parents' lips, not one syllable.

Nothing.

They won't save me.

Because I am nothing to them.

"Wow. That's cold," Fox exclaims.

He was truly expecting them to give in.

Idiot.

He snaps his fingers at the officer, and that one calls the guards back into the room.

"Take them out of my sight," Fox hisses with disgust.

My mother's gaze meets mine one last time, and one single tear falls down her cheek.

"I'm sorry," she mouths.

She's not sorry enough to save me.

She doesn't love me enough to try and prevent this.

I hate her!

Chapter 3

I'm on the bed in my cell, lying on my stomach.

In pain.

So much pain.

My chest, my abs, and my arms are slashed with cuts.

I've been here for over two weeks now. Two weeks and five days, to be precise.

They ran their scalpels through my flesh, and my heart almost stopped under the shock. Sadly, my heart didn't stop for good.

I don't know how much more my carcass can take before it finally gives up. But Death has been ignoring my pleas. And every day, Fox invents new ways to torture me.

I haven't caved in yet.

I'm still waiting for Death to come and free me.

Fox laughed in my face as if reading my thoughts yesterday. He said Death was too busy to bother with someone as pathetic as me.

Or maybe those were the voices talking.

I can't tell the difference anymore.

Life has brought a new monster into existence, and somehow this one is even worse than my father.

I'm not revealing Chi's location.

I didn't face all the pain in my life to give up now.

They can go to hell. They can drag me down there along with them, too.

The door opens and the guard's here. The same asshole who comes here every day to drag me out.

There used to be three of them.

I used to fight them.

I used to struggle.

I used to resist.

That was when my body was still cooperating.

Back when I was still able to move.

I'm so weakened that only one of them is needed to restrain me anymore.

I don't have the strength to walk. The guard just lugs me around like a sack of blood.

I close my eyes and pretend he's not here, but that doesn't prevent him from pulling me off the bed and forcing me out.

Whatever they have reserved for me today, I will take it.

I will *not* cave in.

Chapter 4

I've stopped counting the days.

I've stopped counting the weeks.

I have no idea how long I've been here.

I just know I can't take the pain anymore.

My mind broke somewhere along the way.

The voices have invaded my head and devoured what little hope I had left.

I'm lying on the bed in my cell. There's no position I can find to ease the pain. My whole body is disfigured, slashed and cut. I refuse to look at it, but I can still feel the sharp, burning sensations of the wounds. All night and day.

They've put me on oral medication to numb the pain, just enough to ensure that my body won't give up too quickly. The meds hardly help. They make me sick. I can't keep any food down.

I've been hallucinating.

I see Willow everywhere.

She always tries to soothe me, but a part of me knows she's not real. I can't find the kind of comfort I need from her.

She's sitting by my side right now, but a part of me knows it's not really her. She whispers in my ear while stroking my hair, telling me I've been good. Telling me I've done well.

She's lying.

Today, my body broke, my soul shattered, and I yielded under the lashes. I couldn't take the torture anymore.

My mind bent under the strain they put my body under, and the information spilled out of my mouth against my will. I tried my best to swallow the words back down, but to no avail. I prayed for Death, and Death spat in my face.

My body had enough. It took control of my mind and forced me to surrender.

You're pathetic.

Now, they know Chi's location. Now, they know Chi is hiding with the Jenisons. But what worries me the most is that I've led them straight to Willow.

I hate myself more than I ever did in my entire life.

I deserve to pay for this.

I deserve to *die* for this.

The agonizing pain running through my body is nothing compared to the torment inside my head.

And I deserve it all.

I've led them to Willow's family, and now she will suffer because of me. Because I'm weak.

Because I never deserved her.

Because I am worthless.

The voices all blend together and I can't tell them apart. They're whispering to me all day long, but I can't make out the words. I push my hands against my ears anyway, but nothing works.

The voices never go away.

Chapter 5

Stephen - Fifteen Years Old

The whole family is here sitting at the dinner table—Mother, Father, Chi, and me.

"I received your report card today," Mother says.

I lift my head and meet her eyes. Of course she's talking to me. I'm the only one going to a regular school since Chi stays at home with her. The poor guy. I can't imagine spending all freaking day long with her. I'd go insane.

"So what?" I ask.

Every time, she finds some reason to pass judgment. She's gonna ignore anything positive and focus on what I did wrong.

"You're failing social studies."

There. Just had to criticize something. It's like second nature to her. She can't help herself. She can't ever be nice.

I ignore her and extend my hand to help myself to a second serving of bass that Chi and I fished earlier in the day. Mother freaked out when she found out we'd been outside together. She just had to ruin everything, like she always does. She tried to guilt-trip us, which worked with

Chi, of course. But not with me. Hardly anyone lives around here. There's no way anyone could have seen us. She's constantly using Chi's paranoia against him, to keep him on a leash she can pull at will. Whereas I don't give a damn what she thinks.

I leer at her as I plunge the fork in the platter of fish.

Mother lifts her hand to stop me, but then her gaze turns to Chi. She knows he's gonna ask me to hand him the plate next. She won't stop Chi from getting more, and she can't show her favoritism. Not like this. Not right to his face.

She knows Chi too well. He can't stand injustice. He gets riled up over the tiniest things sometimes. There's this anger deep inside him that's always looking for a trigger, always looking for a target. I've seen him ball his fists, ready to punch a hole in the wall just from watching the news on TV. Mother knows he'll freak out if she treats me unfairly. That's just who he is.

My eyes shift from Chi to Mother, and I smirk at her. Her face hardens, but she doesn't make a sound. She throws me imaginary daggers that have long stopped stabbing mc.

My hand tightens around the fork as I take some more bass.

One ration.

Two rations.

I look at her and smile as I serve myself one more ration. I leave just enough for Chi, but not enough for our parents. Mother knows I did it on purpose. But she won't say *anything because then Chi won't eat his share. He will leave it for them. She squints her eyes at me in anger.*

"Are you going to explain your grades to us?" she asks harshly. "Or do I need to make sure you're doing your homework from now on? For sure you know how to read and write on your own, Stephen. You don't need my supervision while you're studying now, do you?"

She means to hurt my feelings. But she sounds ridiculous. Of course I can write and read!

"They only teach us lies," I retort. "I'm not gonna rot my brain like all those morons at school! Do you know what they said in class today, Mother? They said women like you don't have any rights. That it's the natural order of the world. Are those the values you want me to learn? Really?" I snort at her with disdain. "I thought you wanted me to think for myself. Well, there you go. I'm thinking for myself. I'm not learning their stupid curriculum."

"Stephen," Father cuts me off, warning me to shut up.

I send a glance at him, and Mother's back stiffens. She hates it when Father pays attention to me. She'll never confront him about it, though. Just me. I'm the one responsible for Father's actions after all. I'm the one tempting Mother's loving husband, drawing him into my bed at night, because it is oh so enjoyable.

I want to flip this table over, but I clench my fists instead. The nails cut through my skin and I wince.

"Stephen," Father says again. His hand reaches out for mine and I pull back instinctively. I don't want him to touch me.

Don't touch me, don't touch me! DON'T TOUCH ME!

His skin brushes mine and the feeling sickens me.

He opens his mouth to talk. I try to focus on his words, but fear is here and all around me. He has cast this dread inside me. With one single touch.

I try not to think about it.

I try not to think about tonight.

I'm just an idiot hoping it will be different this time. I'm hoping it'll be one of those nights when he doesn't come to my room.

But any time he doesn't show up at my door, I stay awake most of the night, dreading the moment I'm gonna hear that damn doorknob turn. I lie in bed, wide awake, expecting him to show his face at any moment. Eventually, I fall asleep. But I'm never at peace. I only breathe when I wake up in the morning and realize he's decided to leave me alone for once.

"Good grades... Maintaining appearances... Make us proud." Father is still talking.

Blah, blah, blah.

Blur, blur, blur.

I inhale sharply and try hard not to snicker, not to roll my eyes, not to shoot some sardonic, mildly insulting reply.

I never engage Father the way I taunt Mother. It's never worth the consequences. Never worth the punishment.

"Yes, Father, I'll try to do better."

I'm lying.

I won't try anything.

I don't give a damn what this stupid state is trying to make us swallow. I don't have time to put up with all the bigotry. I don't have the patience for it either.

I have better things to do, like go to Willow, drink her in, and find some kind of peace. Even if it never lasts long enough.

I finish my food and ask if I may be excused. Father nods and smiles at me—a grin filled with promises.

My skin crawls.

I can't breathe.

I need out of here, now.

I head straight to my room, slam the door behind me, and lean against it.

I don't know how long I remain like this. But then someone knocks on my door. I open my eyes in a panic.

Is it nighttime already?

Is he here?

No. No. It's still daylight outside.

I take a breath, step aside, and open a crack between the door and the wall.

Chi.

It's only Chi.

I exhale in relief and let him in.

You need to tell him. Chi needs to know about Father.

No, he can never find out.

Pathetic wimp! Chicken, chicken, chicken! Too scared to tell your own brother!

Shut up!

He won't believe me. He loves them too much. He'll blame me, just like Mother did.

I can't lose him.

I can't afford to lose him over this.

I don't want him to see me like some piece of damaged goods, some broken thing he has to fix. I'd rather he hated me than pitied me. He can never know and I will make sure he never finds out.

Chapter 6

The guard pulls me out of my cell. Fox must have some news for me.

They must have found Chi. He might even be here.

I sure as hell hope not.

When the guard forces me into the interrogation room—that place that sends chills of terror through me—nobody is there but Fox.

He's sitting in a chair, and he raises an eyebrow at me when I walk in. The guard pushes me forward, and I almost stumble as he forces me down, cuffing my arms and legs to the chair. I can't rest my back against it. The wounds are too deep. I can't even stand the fabric of my shirt against my skin. Sitting on my thighs is excruciating, too.

There isn't a part of me they haven't cut through.

Except for my face. For some reason, they never touched my face.

Fox narrows his eyes and strokes his bottom lip back and forth with his index finger as if he's reflecting. But I know better.

This is him acting.

This is him setting the stage for my ultimate destruction.

He looks me deep in the eye and frowns with annoyance.

Something's wrong.

"Mr. Richards." He tsks at me while shaking his head like I'm a child to be scolded. He reminds me of Mother, and I could just spit in his face.

"Why did you lie to us, Stephen?" he asks.

I blink at him. *What is he talking about?*

He pauses and watches my reactions. A few seconds pass by.

"Aww, Stephen, you truly thought your brother was hiding with that family?"

He smirks at me.

I don't respond. I don't nod. I don't understand.

What's going on?

"When we arrived at the location you gave us, your brother wasn't there, Stephen. In fact, those people hadn't seen him in weeks."

This can't be. Mother told us to ask Willow's family for refuge if anything bad ever happened.

She lied to you like she always does. She never meant to save you.

Mother never meant for Chi to hide there.

I should be upset that she lied to me. But that would be me not knowing her as well as I do.

Of course, she would tell Chi to hide in a place I didn't know about. To protect him and keep him safe. From me.

She did it on purpose to punish you. Now you've given away Willow's location over nothing. Chi wasn't even there.

My heart concaves upon itself. Even Mother wouldn't be that twisted and cruel.

Oh, but you know she is.

I force my raspy voice out of my throat. "What about the family?"

I want to ask about Willow more specifically, but they can never know how I feel about her.

"Turns out that family also had one child too many. Were you aware of that, Stephen?"

My heart aches. They know about her. They know about Willow.

I want to scream. I want to ask what they did with her. I want to know where she is.

But I don't say anything.

I feign indifference.

If Fox thinks I don't care, he might not hurt her.

She's an Unwanted. What do you think he's gonna do to her, genius?

"That has been rectified, however," Fox says with detachment.

My heart shatters. My soul breaks.

I almost choke on bile.

But I manage to keep my voice steady. "What do you mean?"

My heart turns cold.

I am ice.

50

I am a wall of ice.

And Fox cannot get through me.

"We disposed of them, of course. New York State doesn't need such traitors, leeches sucking on our system."

You killed her.

Fox is an ice pick striking through my wall. He's reaching for my heart, grasping it, and squeezing it tightly. Pieces of ice fall all around me. My protective wall breaks. And a part of me dies.

The part of me that was still human.

The part of me that still cared.

The part of me that still felt anything at all.

Just died.

In the one second it took for him to tell me that Willow is gone.

You killed her. You killed her!

"You may return to your cell now, Stephen. You are still of use to us. You will be trained. Your loyalty will be tested. I would advise you not to double-cross us. We have more pain reserved for turncoats than we do for the Unwanted."

She died because of you.

You did this.

You destroyed her.

What have I done?!

Chapter 7

She's here. Willow is here. She's running her fingertips over my tortured flesh. Tears well up in her big blue eyes and flow down her soft, freckled cheeks.

"What have they done to you, Stevie?" she asks in a choked-up whisper.

She's crying while looking at the long lacerations on my back. I want to reach her. I need to hold her.

I'm okay. I'm fine.

Please don't cry, Willow. I'm fine.

I reach out for her, but when I try to touch her, my hand goes right through her body.

She's not here. This isn't real, you gullible fool.

I know that. I just need to pretend.

I can't.

I can't deal with this reality right now.

They took her away from me.

But maybe the medication can bring her back to me.

Maybe I can hallucinate her presence into reality.

If only my mind could break just slightly more.

I could give in to lunacy.

I could be with her for good.

I choose insanity over rationality. Because madness might drive this pain away.

But Willow is still crying and I'm aching inside and out.

All over.

Nothing but pain.

I try to turn around and lie on my back. The slashes hurt me so much I can't. I can't lie down that way.

I turn to the side. That doesn't help either.

Her image slowly fades away and I try to hold on.

Please, don't go. Don't leave me. Please don't leave me here like this. I need you. Willow, I need you.

I try to hold her back, but she's gone. She's gone and a deep wail of pain escapes my throat.

Willow, I love you. Please, don't leave me.

Willow is dead. You killed her. She died because of you.

I push my face against the mattress to quiet down the sounds of my agony. I don't want them to hear me. I don't want them to know this is worse than any physical pain they could ever put me through.

I'm crying and screaming my rage. My face buried in the mattress.

I cry and holler against the mattress until I suffocate.

Until it all turns dark.

Until I faint.

Chapter 8

Stephen - Sixteen Years Old

I'm sitting on a branch in the tree outside *Willow's bedroom. I'm ready to knock on her window, but first, I steal a glance around to make sure no one can see me.*

The room looks dark behind her curtains. She's probably asleep. I shouldn't wake her up, but I haven't seen her in a week and I miss her. I knock a couple of times.

The light turns on. I knock once more and whisper her name. I don't want to freak her out. She might think I'm some psycho lurking outside, trying to break in. I've never done this before and we've never discussed my coming here.

She pushes one curtain slightly to the side, and I move so the moonlight shines down on my face.

She blinks a few times and rubs her left eye with one fist while yawning with her mouth wide open.

This has gotta be the cutest thing I've ever seen.

I can't help but smile.

Damn it, I just want to hug her.

I beam at her as she works on opening the window.

"Stevie, is that you?" she asks.

"Yeah."

She blinks again.

"What are you doing here?"

"You never showed up this week," I answer.

"I'm sorry, Stevie. Mom has kept me busy. We were trying to keep the chickens comfortable in the heat."

"Can I come in?" I ask.

She gives me a shy smile and bats her lashes.

Damn, she's so cute.

She doesn't even know how freaking cute she is.

"Okay," she finally replies.

The tree is close to the house, making it easy for me to enter her room. My feet hit the carpeted floor as she closes the window and curtain quickly.

"Dad will kill you if he finds you here," she whispers, a hard blush coloring her cheeks.

I cup her face and kiss her on the nose.

"I won't stay for long."

That's a lie. I plan on staying for as long as she'll let me.

She covers her mouth with her hand and giggles.

"You're just looking for trouble," she says and bites her lower lip.

She has no idea how much trouble I wanna get into when it comes to her.

The things I wanna do with her, to her. She has no idea.

I pull her to me. "I've missed you."

I kiss her, slowly at first, and then more deeply. Her fingers play with the hair at the nape of my neck, and it takes all I've got not to groan. I pull her closer and graze her mouth open with my tongue until our kiss deepens.

Her lavender scent surrounds me. It makes me dizzy. She's killing me, really. I pull back just slightly so she can't feel what her touch is doing to me. She's not ready. Though I never asked, I keep telling myself she's not ready. I can't push for more.

I pull away and take in her room. I've never been here before. The walls are a pale shade of green, decorated with dried flowers of all shapes and colors.

I let go of her and walk around. I look at each flower that she has found, dried, and carefully framed behind glass. Multiple drawings are nailed to a cork board above the desk facing her bed.

"Why didn't you frame those?" I ask.

"Oh you know, they're just drawings," she answers without explaining why she cares more about dead flowers than these beautiful pictures.

"Did you make them?"

She nods at me and bites her upper lip.

"They're beautiful, sweetheart."

"Thank you." She flushes, and I extend my hand out to her. She takes a step forward, intertwines her fingers with mine, and I pull her by my side.

I lean over her desk while holding her waist against mine. I want to see the drawings more closely. All of them represent animals—squirrels, snails, owls.

Detailed. Delicate. Beautiful. Just like Willow.

56

I notice a pad on her desk and point to it. "Do you have more in here?"

She nods silently.

"May I look?"

She nods again.

I open the first page, to find a myriad of fish. Colorful fish. Some red, some orange, some purple.

The next page represents an animal I've never seen before. Its long arms end in impressive claws that could probably kill just about anything.

"What animal is this?" I ask Willow.

She turns her turquoise blue eyes to me and her smile spreads, beaming at me. Her entire face illuminates like it does any time we're about to discuss an animal she truly loves.

"It's a sloth."

"A sloth, huh? Does it sleep all day or something?"

She chuckles. "They are very slow animals."

"Ah." I run my fingers over the paper.

Willow pulls away from me and grabs a book from the shelf above her desk. I recognize it as the animal encyclopedia I gave her a couple of months ago. Mother still hasn't found out that it's missing—proof enough that Willow needs it more than Mother does. Willow doesn't know where the book came from. She thinks I bought it in a store in downtown Eboracum City. She doesn't know encyclopedias are actually rare and illegal to possess. She also doesn't know I've never been to the city. My parents can't afford to be spotted strolling around that area. It's dangerous enough for me to go to school and Father to go to work.

Willow opens the book and looks through the table of contents. When she finds what she's looking for, she turns more pages and shows me the animal in question. Not just a drawing this time, but a real picture of it.

"I wonder if they still exist," I say.

"I don't know," she replies sadly.

I nod and kiss her temple.

"Wouldn't it be incredible to see one someday?" I ask, to distract her.

This animal is probably extinct, like so many others—a morbid reality that usually brings Willow to tears. I don't want her to cry. Not tonight. Not ever.

"Yes," she says, brightening up again. She nods her head over and over again with enthusiasm. I kiss her hair.

She leans her head against my shoulder and wraps her arms around my waist as I flip through a few more pages of her pad. Until I stop.

A picture of my face is staring right back at me.

I blink, but the picture doesn't go away.

Willows gasps and tries to close the pad, but I keep my hand on it to keep it open.

"Is this me?" I ask.

She doesn't reply. She doesn't nod. Her cheeks blossom into a deep reddish pink like cherry buds blooming on her face.

"When did you make this?" I whisper in her ear.

"A few months ago," she replies in a low, timid voice.

"Would you make a picture of yourself? I mean, would you draw yourself for me?"

She looks at me and smiles. "If you want me to."

I close the pad and turn her around so she's facing me. I bend over to kiss her neck, and she giggles delightfully.

I kiss her neck once more, just to hear her giggle again.

"Can I stay a bit longer?" I ask against the skin of her throat.

"Yes."

I press her body against the desk and she flushes hard. I kiss her. I kiss her until I can't breathe and the room starts spinning.

When I pull away, something catches my eye—an aquarium on a small table by her desk. I hadn't noticed it until now because I was too mesmerized by her drawings.

"What's in the aquarium?" I ask.

"Oh, that's just Toadette," she replies.

I squint my eyes, and she moves past me to reach the aquarium.

"She looked really sick when I found her," she says. "She should be able to go back out soon. But I'm selfish and I want to keep her for myself. I don't want her to leave. But I'll be happy once I no longer have to feed her. I don't like it when she eats the insects."

I send Willow a glance and approach the small table.

"Toadette. Toadette, come out, sweetie-pie," Willow whispers while peeking through the transparent top of the aquarium.

I'm about to tap on the glass when she grabs my wrist.

"Don't do that. You're going to scare her. She doesn't like it when people bother her."

"How do you know it's a female?" I ask.

"She's not an 'it,' and I know because she's really cuddly," she replies as if that explains anything.

She opens the top and I wince when a huge, ugly toad gets out from where it was hiding underneath some leaves.

"Please, don't take it out," I say, almost like a reflex.

Willow sends me a quick look and chuckles. "No need to be scared, Stevie. She's really nice."

I take a step back. "Please, don't take her out. I can see her perfectly well from here."

Nasty beast that she is! Gross!

Willow giggles as she closes the top and looks at me, her kind eyes turning playful.

"I didn't think you'd be so scared of a little toad, Stevie," she teases.

"Little is an overstatement here. Besides, I'm not scared at all," I reply to save face. I just don't want that thing anywhere near my skin. "I thought toads gave warts."

Willow smiles at me and shows me her fingertips. "You just need to wash your hands."

I take another step back and she takes one step forward, and then two, and then three. She stands in front of me and gets on her tiptoes to kiss me on the nose.

"You're so cute when you're scared," she whispers against my cheek, and the air from her mouth on my skin makes me shiver.

I smile at her, take her hand in mine, and lead her to her bed. She's looking at me the entire time, with her big blue eyes wide open, studying me.

I let her lie down and settle next to her. She pushes her tiny frame against mine, with her arm over my stomach and her cheek on my collarbone.

"Stevie?"

"Yes, sweetheart."

"Would you come here again tomorrow night?" she asks.

"You want me to?"

She nods against my chest.

"Well then yes, I will."

I smile at her, stroke her hair, and kiss her forehead. I wish I could spend every night here. I love it here. I hate my room—that dreadful place.

But I won't be able to come here right away. Father can't know I sneaked out. I can't risk that. I remember what he did to me the one time he came to my room and found my bed empty. I was only ten years old back then. I'd managed to convince Chi to let me spend the night in his room instead. I hid from Father and it seemed like a smart plan at the time,

Alice Rachel

but the next day Father made me pay double the price and I never tried to hide from him again after that.

Father can't find out about Willow. I'll just have to wait until he's done before I can come here.

I shudder.

"Stevie, are you cold?" Willow asks, rubbing my arm to warm me up.

I shake my head and force a smile on my face.

I don't want to think about Father right now. I never want to think about him when I'm with her.

I pull her closer and notice two books on her nightstand table. My Side of the Mountain and Peter Rabbit. I gave those to Willow as presents two weeks ago. Mother is going to throw a fit if she sees I stole some of her books again. I don't know why Mother bothered to bring those along when we lost everything in the move. They probably belonged to Chi when we were little. I don't care. Willow deserves the books more than Chi does.

"Did you like them?" I ask her, pointing at the books.

She nods with glee. "Yes, they're my favorites. I just love Peter Rabbit."

"Why do you like him so much?" I ask.

She giggles. "He's very naughty. He never does what he's told. Just like you."

I chuckle and raise my eyebrow at her. "You like that, huh?"

"Yes," she replies. Her cheeks blossom into red again, and she nestles closer against my chest.

62

She falls asleep eventually and we remain like this for a while. I look down at her and stroke her hair. In her arms, I feel safe—a calm sensation that only comes when I'm with her. Willow would never let anyone hurt me. She's the only reason why I'm still alive, the only reason why I still care to breathe, and she doesn't even know what her love means to me. I close my eyes.

Willow would hate Father for what he does to you at night.

Willow is incapable of hate. And I refuse to cast this kind of darkness into her heart.

At some point, I slip out from underneath her and pull the sheets up to cover her. She's wearing nothing but a light blue sleeping gown.

She's so beautiful.

I look at her for a while longer. Sleeping Willow is such a peaceful sight in my violent, ugly world.

I turn off the light and get out the same way I came in. I don't want her parents to find us together. The last thing she needs is for me to bring this kind of trouble into her life.

Chapter 9

Stephen - Eighteen Years Old

It's been six months and twenty-five days since Willow passed away.

Six months and twenty-five days since they took her from me.

Six months and twenty-five days since I stopped being human.

They've been training me. Every day, they teach me how to shoot, how to defend myself. They treat me like shit. That would probably hurt my feelings if I had any left. But my heart has hardened over the months. And I feel nothing.

I care about nothing.

I go through the motions.

How they trust me to hold a gun and not shoot Fox, I don't know.

He's a fool if he thinks I won't make him pay the price for his sins.

He's a fool if he believes I will ever forget.

It's been six months and twenty-six days since they last cut through my flesh.

The wounds slowly healed over time. They itched all over my body for so long. Now they are just remnants of what I've done. Of what I still have to pay for, even if I know there's no way for me to make amends.

I'm lying on my bed, waiting for the clicking sound. The sound telling me they've automatically unlocked the door. The sound announcing more training, more of me dragging my carcass around this place like I give a damn what Fox wants from me.

But the sound is different today. And I recognize it instantly as the sound of a guard unlocking the door with a key. A guard coming for me.

The door opens and the guard walks in.

I stare at the person.

She's a girl. A young woman.

And she's not a guard. Nor is she a regular camp officer. She's a chief civil officer, dressed entirely in black. The insignia on her chest is proof enough of her rank. I've only seen one chief civil officer around here so far. They are the most dreaded by the population, the most ruthless, the most deadly. I've never met a female officer before—not even a female guard. Fox only employs men for those jobs—or so I thought.

The girl is about my age, maybe a few years older. How she managed to reach such a high position is beyond me.

She steps in, and when she sees me, she stops in her tracks. She blinks a few times. She doesn't move. She just blinks. She's looking at me like she's seen a ghost.

I return her gaze and frown. *What's her deal?*

"What?"

"You look just like him," she says. "Of course, I knew that, but..." She catches herself, but too late. She has revealed something she shouldn't have.

She blushes.

Too late.

There's only one person in this world who looks like me.

Chi.

I wince.

"Do you know my brother?" I ask.

She doesn't answer.

She blushes more profusely and I lose patience.

"Answer me."

She stutters, "I...I don't know what you're talking about."

"Do you know where he is?"

She doesn't answer.

"Never mind. I don't wanna know. If you say anything, they'll pull the information out of me."

I wait for her reaction, but she gives me none, except for her cheeks reddening more deeply when I talk about him. She's averting her eyes too as if she can't quite face me. Her attitude tells me more than she thinks she's letting on.

This beautiful blonde girl likes Chi—a lot. And probably as more than just a friend, too. *How did she get to know him? Where is he staying?*

"Is Chi okay?" I ask and pretend not to notice her discomfort when I say his name.

"Yes." One simple word to confirm that she knows him, that she knows where he is. I don't need to know more than that.

I don't want to know more than that.

"Who are you?" I inquire.

I give her a simple once-over. She's fair-skinned, short and petite—incredibly petite. Her hair is long, pulled back in a ponytail under her black peaked cap, and her eyes are dark blue.

I ask again who she is, and she hesitates. She has revealed too much already and she knows it.

"Don't worry," I try to reassure her. "I won't tell anyone that you know where Chi is."

"Are you really his brother?" she asks.

"Isn't my face proof enough?"

She watches me as I stretch my arms lazily over my head and get off the bed.

"Did he talk about me?" I ask as I grab the gray vest I have to wear as a trainee. I pull it off the back of the chair and put it on while observing the girl from the corner of my eye.

"Once," she replies.

So little brother does remember I exist. *How interesting!*

"Is he looking for me?"

She doesn't reply right away.

"He's looking for your parents," she says eventually.

Her words are like needles piercing through my scarred skin. And disappointment seeps in through my veins, all the way to my heart.

Of course. *What was I expecting?*

Chi thinks I'm a monster. He's probably relieved that I'm gone.

"I see." I feign indifference.

Her eyes squint slightly. I'm not fooling her.

"You never told me your name," I say again.

"I'm Tina," she replies.

"I'm—"

"Stephen. I know."

So Chi has talked about me long enough for her to remember my name. I'm almost flattered. I'm surprised he's mentioned me at all. I'm the ugly duckling he's always tried to hide. I wonder how he's portrayed me. Not kindly, I'm sure.

Tina doesn't seem to fear me, though. She's just staring at me like I'm some specimen to be evaluated.

"Chi has mentioned you a few times. He's been looking for you as well."

Really? Who would have thought? Maybe little bro does care about me after all.

Yeah, keep on telling yourself that!

Her gaze shifts and her eyes travel around my sparkling clean cell. This place was a shit hole when I arrived. Fox said I was in charge of cleaning said shit hole, so I did. That's the one trait I've inherited from Mother—the need to tidy and clean and organize everything. When you can't control people's actions around you, you grow this urge to control anything else you can.

Tina takes in the walls that have no windows, the tiled floor that I scrubbed until it shone again. She has quickly toured the tiny cell I've been forced to live in. The bathroom is even smaller, with nothing but a sink, a shower, and a toilet—all crammed into the tiniest space it could all fit in.

"Why are you here, Tina?" I ask.

Something flickers through her eyes. She had forgotten why she was here.

"Mr. Fox wants to see you. It's time for your test," she says and casts me a sad look.

One single shiver shoots through my spine.

Chapter 10

Tina brings me to the courtyard. Fox is there, along with six other officers and four trainees waiting for their final test.

A family is standing with their backs propped against a wall. A man, a woman, and three children.

Three children who all look identical.

No family is allowed to have three kids. Especially not since the Sterilization Law was passed.

These children are illegals, Unwanted, like Chi.

I steal a glance at them before giving Fox my full attention. His back is turned to me and he's talking to the four trainees, but he moves around and looks at me when he hears me coming.

"Stephen," he calls my name, all cheerful as if he's truly excited to see me. This doesn't bode well. Whatever he has planned, I'm going to hate it. His smile is too wide, too fake, too full of white teeth. He reeks of something impure and evil.

I look him straight in the eyes.

Someday, I will kill you, asshole.

Someday, you will beg for my mercy.

I will make you pay for what you did to Willow.

I crack my vertebrae, and Fox's smile falters when I glare at him. He hesitates for just one second. One single second during which actual fear crosses his eyes. He knows not to trust me. Maybe he's smarter than I gave him credit for.

But he quickly pastes another fake smile on his face. And I want to hurl at his feet. *What a grotesque excuse for a human being!*

I can't hide the revulsion he always triggers inside me.

"Stephen, please do not disappoint me this time," Fox says. He never forgot how much torture it took for me to finally cave in and reveal where I thought Chi was hiding.

"See, this test is very simple," he adds. "This family thought they could breed more than our government allows. More than we can take. They deserve punishment. I want these three children removed."

The parents gasp and gather around their kids to shield them from us, but two officers pry them apart.

I don't respond.

If Fox thinks I'm gonna agree to this, he's a freaking moron.

I'm not gonna kill a bunch of innocent kids just because some buffoon told me to.

I stare at the idiot without blinking. I want to ask him how freaking stupid he truly is, but I keep my mouth shut.

If they're dumb enough to put a weapon in my hands, I will shoot him first, his officers second.

I don't care if they respond. I don't care if one of their bullets hits me.

I don't care if they shoot me dead either.

This is the chance I've been waiting for.

This is the chance I'm taking.

"There is one prisoner here for each one of you. I want you to shoot each child and both parents. One bullet in each one of their skulls. That simple." He shrugs as if killing innocent kids was truly that simple. Maybe to him it is.

An officer hands me a gun. The other trainees are already standing in position, with their rifles raised toward the family. I count the odds working against me—Fox, six officers, four trainees apparently willing to shoot whoever they have to in order to get a stupid job, and maybe Tina if she's on their side. I won't be able to take them all down. Fox is my main goal, the ultimate target.

I join the other morons already standing in killing mode.

The kids in front of us quiver and shake in fear, with their backs pressed against the wall.

I want to throw up.

I clench my jaw.

I grip the weapon tightly.

I point it at them and their reactions throw a tremor all the way down my spine.

Fox counts out with his fingers raised.

"Three."

"Two."

"One."

I shift gear.

And I shoot.

The bullet hits Fox in the shoulder.

I missed my target. I was aiming for his heart.

He stumbles backward, and electricity hits me hard.

I can't move.

I fall down.

I hit the ground and my body convulses.

I try to regain control, but I'm paralyzed.

They're tasing me.

Fox groans. His shirt is covered with blood.

He glares at me. I would laugh, but my body is twitching and I can't do anything.

The other trainees haven't fired their guns yet. I can feel them behind my back, standing there, staring at me.

I'm gonna pay a high price for humiliating Fox.

He signals for the officers to finish the job.

Gunshots echo through the yard, deafening me. The kids' small bodies fall to the ground and the parents' wails of sorrow resound, soon followed by sobs of misery, then more gunshots. The parents fall and I throw up right there on the pavement.

My heart turns a little bit colder than it already was.

And I add tonight to the list of things.

The list of things Fox will pay for eventually.

For each child that he killed tonight, he will pay tenfold.

His officers grab my armpits and drag me away.

I glance at Tina.

Her eyes meet mine.

She's staring at me, with her eyes and her mouth wide open in awe and horror. Until she looks away and feigns indifference.

Chapter 11

They've kept me on this chair all day.

But then, Fox finally makes his entrance.

His arm is in a sling.

I can't stop the grin from spreading on my face.

He looks at me, his eyes two murderous orbits of deep forest green. My sneer widens. I've managed to piss him off.

Not quite what I wanted. But that'll have to do for now.

Next time, I'll make sure not to miss.

Next time, I'll shoot him straight in the heart.

He walks to me and towers over my seat. But he doesn't impress me.

I've managed to shatter some of his pride.

He wasn't expecting that. Proof enough that he's a profound idiot.

"You failed your test, Mr. Richards," he says, his voice filled with disgust.

"Oh, did I?" I snicker arrogantly.

"Don't play that little game with me, Stephen. I can guarantee you that you will lose."

I smirk again. *What is he gonna do to me now?*

"Don't be so snide, young man. I can make your misery last longer than you can bear, trust me."

I keep my grin on. He has already wrecked havoc on my body, so much so that I don't even recognize myself in the mirror. *Am I supposed to be scared?*

Maybe I'm just a fool for no longer fearing him. But he disgusts me so much that my revulsion blurs all sense of reason.

Fox tilts his head toward the officer who's been standing guard by the door.

"Let's get this started, shall we?"

Chapter 12

Fox had quite the punishment planned for me. A whole new series of sadistic sessions.

Each day, two of his guards pull me out of my cell.

And each day, they run small flames over my flesh.

Matches and candles, wax and acid. Boiling water.

Each day, the smell of burnt flesh rises to prickle my nose and make me puke.

Each day, agony seizes me by the core as unbearable pain hits my nerves.

This is what hell must be like. Each day, every day.

But Fox is getting bored.

After two days, he gets tired of torturing me and no longer attends the sessions. His brainless dogs do the job for him instead.

After six days, he finally makes an appearance to tell me this was the last session and that he hopes I've learned my lesson.

Yes, I've learned my lesson all right.

I've learned he's a sadistic asshole.

I've learned there is no threshold to the amount of hatred I can feel for someone like him.

I've learned not to miss my target next time.

But I've resolved myself to behave despite my strong desire to burn this whole place to the ground.

I need to prove to that jerk that I can be trusted. I will comply and infiltrate his system until the moment is right, until I get another chance, until I destroy him for good.

I will endure anything they put me through, with that single goal in mind. Everything he may ask for, I will do.

To a certain point.

Even I still have standards for myself. Even I have a limit to what I'm willing to accept.

Chapter 13

Stephen - Nineteen Years Old

It's been one year, two weeks, and six days since Willow died because of me.

The things I've done since then fill me with shame. I can't imagine what Willow would think of me. She would hate everything I've had to do.

Everything I've become.

Everything I am today.

And who could blame her? I hate myself, too.

Guarding this camp is a crime I will pay for eventually.

I've done what I have to if I am to take Fox down someday. After Fox's dogs burned my skin over a year ago, Fox forced me through more training. I had to accomplish the final test. He promised me a bullet in the head if I didn't comply.

I am no longer just a prisoner held against my will.

I am now also a guard working against my will.

Fox put me in the apicultural area. He told me he was willing to set our past "incident" behind us and move on.

He's an idiot. I will never move on. I will never forget. I will never forgive.

Every day, I stand on a bridge with two other guards and one camp officer. I overlook the prisoners who work with bees to collect their honey. The officer is the one in charge. The other guards and I are mere puppets obeying him, making sure the prisoners do their job. Like I give a shit if this camp makes profit or not.

Fox doesn't trust me to carry a gun anywhere near him anymore. He's a moron if he thinks that will stop me.

He doesn't trust me enough to ever let me leave the camp either. Unlike my co-workers, I don't get to have a normal life outside these walls.

So I pretend I like this stupid job. I pretend I was meant for this.

The things I've done, I shall burn in hell for.

But my ultimate goal hasn't changed.

Fox is still my final target.

For months, he wouldn't let me have a weapon at all. I had to crawl at his feet like some pathetic wimp to prove I was worthy. He finally let me carry a rifle about three months ago, for lack of another choice. The prisoners need to fear me if they are to accomplish their tasks, hence the stupid gun in my hands.

The apicultural room is locked from the inside, with a code that Fox failed to give me. If I shoot someone, I won't make it out. And every day, the officer takes my gun away before I leave this place. Fox is cautious, I'll give him that.

Not that it'll save his skin. As far as I'm concerned, he's a dead carcass already. It's only a matter of time and opportunity before I get rid of him for good.

He took the only person I ever cared about.

And every day, a part of me withers away.

I am all thorns.

I am all pain.

I am all hatred.

I am pure loathing.

The only things I ever let myself feel anymore are self-disgust and repugnance. I'm carrying so much revulsion that it burns right through my veins.

It gives me fuel. It helps me focus on the ultimate goal: Fox's death as sole retribution.

My life is a nightmare I cannot escape.

And my soul has long left this corpse I still inhabit.

It has deserted this ship and my heart has frozen over.

Everything that made me human is now gone.

Chapter 14

Over the months, Tina has managed to break a part of my wall and find her way under my shield. She's the only person I've befriended around this place. In spite of my resolution not to get close to anyone, in spite of everything, she has worked her way into my life.

She's here on certain days only.

She works outside of the camp mostly.

She and I spend time together when we can, which is not often.

"How did you get the job?" I ask her one day. "You're the only female officer I know."

"That's because I'm the only female officer, period," she replies. "Well, at least in this area, and that I'm aware of."

"How did you get promoted?"

"I don't think you really want to know," she replies, looking away sadly.

"How come you're in this camp every week if you work on the outside?"

She sighs deeply. "I'm an informant for Fox. I have to report to him weekly with information I may or may not have gathered about the rebels in the area."

Tina tells me she's a double agent, a spy for the Underground—the exact same rebel group my parents mentioned a few times when Chi and I were little. Fox doesn't know she's on their side. He believes she's working in his favor. *How much dumber can the guy get?*

Tina hates her job here, just like I do. But the outcome is worth the sacrifice, I guess.

I move from where I was lying on my bed and sit on the edge so I can look at her as I talk.

"I don't understand why he sent you to come get me for the test that day," I say. "He usually sends his guards."

She sends me a tiny smile coupled with a weak shrug. "I was there and my insignia impresses people. He warned me you'd be reluctant."

I watch her for a beat as she stands up from her chair and comes to sit by my side. She looks me in the eyes, without a smile or a single emotion coming through, until her gaze shifts to my exposed arms and a flicker of pain flashes through her cobalt stare. Her hand reaches out tentatively and she runs her fingertips over the burns.

I wince and pull away.

She apologizes.

The scars don't hurt anymore, really. It's just a reflex I have.

I hate it when she touches my scars.

I hate it when anyone sees my scars.

Her hand moves toward them again and I flinch instinctively. She pauses and holds her palm right above my skin before bringing it down against my tortured flesh.

I let her.

She caresses the cuts with her index finger.

"Did they do that to you as well?" she asks while stroking the slashes.

She already knows what it cost me that day when I refused to shoot the kids. She was there when they brought me back to my cell after burning my flesh.

I can hear the pity in her tone and I hate it instantly.

"Yeah, they did." I pull my arm away and look at it. I inspect the lacerations. They've turned pale now, but they're still visible.

I hate them.

I hate the scars.

I hate that my ugliness is now apparent to the world.

I can no longer hide it within.

It is plain for all to see.

They've carved it into my skin so I can no longer hide what a monster I truly am.

And the pity in her eyes, I don't want to see it. I don't deserve it.

She moves closer and pulls my face toward hers. Her palm is soft against my cheek, so I close my eyes and lean into it.

"Stephen," she says, but I don't respond.

She shifts closer, her breath now tickling my skin. When her lips brush against mine, just once, my eyes fly open. Her gaze is on me, studying me, watching my reactions.

I try to turn my face away, but her hand is in my hair and she's pulling me to her again. Her mouth covers mine, parting my lips with hers, and though I know I should push her back, I don't.

"I just want to kiss you," she says against my mouth.

Her lips are soft and she tastes like strawberries.

When she pulls back, her eyes search through mine, reaching out for my soul, but she won't find it there. My soul left this place a long time ago.

Her lips come crashing against mine again.

And I let her kiss me. My body surrenders.

Until I come to my senses and push her away. "I can't."

She kisses me again, with more insistence. Her lips quiver against mine, but I don't return her gesture this time. I push her back.

"Don't."

She looks at me and something takes flight in her eyes, present one second, gone the next. I see all her feelings fluttering through the expressions of her face: her pain, her sadness, her anger maybe? Before she shuts them all down and looks away.

"Why not?" she asks with insecurity and aggravation growling through her tone.

"Whatever it is you want from me, I can't give it to you," I reply.

I'm not getting involved with anyone—not today, not tomorrow, not ever again.

Love is gone for good. It has left this barren place behind, abandoning my heart, this widening hole.

Push her away, you don't deserve her.

"How can you deny me something I didn't even ask for?" she asks, with irritation floating through her voice. "You have no idea what I want."

She's right. I don't know. I'm just guessing.

"Oh, I have an idea all right," I reply just to spite her.

"You're a conceited jerk, you know that?" she exclaims, rising to her feet. She turns her back to me, crossing her arms over her chest.

She's pouting. It's cute.

I try to hide my cocky smile. And fail.

She's too adorable.

She's upset, though, and a part of me cares.

She's the only person who's treated me like an actual human being since I got here.

But if I give in, I will hurt her more than she knows.

I always hurt those around me—always.

That's who I am.

That's what I do.

That's the package I carry; that's what I drag along.

And if Fox thinks I'm even remotely interested in Tina, he will use her against me. He will make her pay and suffer. He will torture her to torment me, to make me yield against my will, to compel me to do things, terrible things I don't want to be forced into.

I want to touch her and comfort her, but that would be me putting her in danger.

She should stay far away from me.

She turns around, her eyes flashing.

"You're just like him," she exclaims with resentment.

And I receive the words like slaps in the face.

She's comparing me.

She's comparing me to *him*.

She's comparing me to Chi.

If she's trying to antagonize me, she's doing a really good job. Anger flares and soon I'm unable to control myself. I'm suddenly so mad that I have to look away and inhale deeply.

I hate being compared to him.

I am *nothing* like him.

He's weak. Too fragile to ever carry this weight I'm bearing.

His innocence, he owes it to me.

The peace in his life, he owes it to me as well.

He's only good because he was given a choice I was denied. He's only better because that chance was bestowed upon him and not me.

I have to shield myself before I use words to spite her, to strike her down and hurt her even more than I already have.

I try to raise the walls around me.

But it's too late. I can't help myself.

The words spill out. I can't stop now. I will slash back at her to push her away until she finally gets the message, until she gets sick of me and lets me be.

"Tell me, Tina," I say. "Is that what this is about? You not being able to get Chi and coming to me as your second option?"

She gasps, but doesn't reply.

I've hit spot on.

She can't fool me.

This isn't about me. This is about Chi.

Our so-called friendship has always been about Chi. This is about her wanting Chi, being denied, and going for the next best thing instead.

Her feelings for him always spill through her voice when she speaks his name. I know the signs. She's so transparent, I'm surprised she actually thought she could fool me, even for one second.

I should be vexed, or hurt, or angry. I know I'm supposed to feel some kind of human emotion right now, but I don't. I don't feel anything.

I'm indifferent.

Numb.

Empty.

I don't want her to get attached to me.

I don't want her to want me.

I don't want her to feel for me.

If she wants to be with me because she can't have him, I'm okay with that. Her using me is fine, actually. I don't deserve better and I truly don't care.

I've been floating in apathy for months, with physical pain for sole company.

I stand up and close the distance between us. I tower over her and cup her face before I pull her into a kiss.

I haven't kissed anyone in almost two years.

But I'm kissing her now. An emotionless brush of my lips against hers.

But I don't feel anything.

I just want and I just take. I don't give anything in return. She's right, I am a jerk.

And she's letting me kiss her. Because this is her using me too, and she knows it.

I pull back.

"I am not him, Tina," I say, still holding her face. I owe it to her to make that clear. "If it's romance you're looking for, I'm not it. If you want someone like him, I'm not it. If you want love, I simply am not it."

My tone is harsh, grinding.

She closes her eyes.

"Why did you kiss me?" I ask, and my voice cracks because I'm upset at her.

I'm upset she kissed me first.

I'm upset she's letting me kiss her back.

This is going nowhere and we both know it.

"I don't know," she replies. "Because you..."

She doesn't finish her sentence.

"Because I look like him," I say. I don't need to ask for her confirmation. I already know. And I don't even resent her.

"This won't work, Tina. I'm not him. I never was and I never will be."

A single tear rolls down her face. "I know. I just—"

I interrupt her again. This time, by pressing my lips against hers desperately. And she lets me.

I have no clue what I'm doing.

I've endured so much pain this past year—horrors no one should ever have to face—and her lips against mine feel like a silver lining.

I take what she's giving me, right here, right now, before she decides to take it back.

And I take it all, even though it's not meant for me.

Even though she wishes I were him.

Even though I will never be enough.

Chapter 15

A few weeks later, the knob turns. It's her.

The door opens and she steps in. She closes it, and I can tell right away that something's wrong. Her face is tear-marked with long red lines running down her cheeks. Black smudges underline her eyes where her makeup has poured down her skin.

For months, she's been visiting me, but I've never seen her this distressed before.

I stand up and take a step toward her.

"What's wrong?"

"He has a girlfriend," she replies. "He told me he couldn't get involved with anyone, but he did—with her." She says the words and they shouldn't affect me, but they do.

Her words almost strike me down to my knees.

Little brother got himself a new girlfriend. Suddenly my past resentment shows its nasty face, growing, swelling through my chest, almost suffocating me.

Anger flares deep inside and hatred grabs me by the throat.

I'm not mad that Tina is upset.

Though she has kissed me more than once before, she has never claimed to want me for me. She's never pretended she didn't love Chi.

I'm not jealous of how she feels about him.

I'm upset because he has replaced Willow.

He's over her.

I'm still here drowning while he has moved on.

And I want to break something.

I want to tear through the walls of my cell.

I want to reach him.

I want to destroy him.

I could kill him.

He's with someone else and I'm about to throw up.

Tina is crying and I'm unable to comfort her.

"They're not even dating or anything," she says. "But she's all he talks about anymore, and he wants to be with her. I can tell he's infatuated with her, and..." She turns around, choking on a sob, ready to leave. "I'm sorry. I shouldn't have come to you about this."

I grab her wrist and stop her. Tina thinks I'm upset with her.

She doesn't understand; my anger runs much deeper.

My rage isn't about her. It's about *him*. It's about Chi.

About how much I hate him for taking Willow away from me, for being with her and not even caring about her.

I pull Tina to my chest and run my thumbs over both her cheeks to wipe her tears away.

A sob rises to rock her body. This is more than I can bear.

Her pain, I can't take it. I can't take it. I don't want to see it.

But it's all I see, all I can feel right now.

It'd been a while since I'd felt this much hatred for Chi, but I want him to hurt so much right now I can't breathe.

Tina pulls me to her with both her hands tugging at my hair. Her lips meet mine and she kisses me hard, with so much greed I can't pull away. Her tongue pries my mouth open with passionate strokes and I could devour her whole.

This pain, I can't take it anymore.

I don't want it anymore.

My vision blurs. I am all need, consumed by sudden, fierce hunger.

I kiss her deeply, my tongue seeking hers over and over again as I pin her against the door and she responds to my touch, her body capitulating and molding to mine.

When I lift her up and hold her in place, she wraps her legs around my waist. Her hands are all over me, in my hair, stroking my shoulders, falling to the small of my back. She pulls me closer, kissing me desperately, pulling at the hair on the nape of my neck. I press her body hard against the door as she reaches for my shirt and pulls it over my head. When she sees the scars marking my chest and abs, she inhales sharply, her reaction stabbing me right where it hurts, hitting me hard with insecurity. Until she whimpers my name and groans against my lips, "You're so beautiful."

Liar.

She outlines my muscles with her fingertips and then the burns and slashes on my skin, one by one. I cup her face again and she clutches my shoulders for support as I cover her mouth with mine and kiss her, harder and harder.

Desire burns right through my veins. I can't think anymore. She moans against me. I'm done for.

Clothes get torn off, thrown, scattered all over the place. And we collide, we crash, we shove, we ache, and we breathe into each other. Desperately begging to be brought back to life, desperately looking for some type of sensation, some type of feeling—anything to take this pain away. This is us tearing at each other right here against the door of my cell, desperately searching for something we know we can't provide each other.

This is us taking revenge. Against the world, against fate, against Chi.

This is me losing myself into her, her using me, and us begging for deliverance from this agony.

And when we're done, we don't feel any better.

She deserves better than that jerk in her life. And she deserves better than me too.

I know that. She knows it too.

This isn't what I wanted. This isn't what she wanted either.

I wanted Willow. She wanted Chi. We settled for the next best thing.

94

After that, we christen every single spot in my cell.

And I just can't get enough.

Eventually, we crash next to each other on my bed. I look at the clock and then at her.

"You should leave."

"I want to stay longer."

She knows it's not wise. She stayed way too long already.

"Leave, please."

She sits up and looks down at me. I hurt her feelings. I didn't mean for it to come out that way. I didn't mean to sound so callous.

"If they find you here, they'll use you against me," I explain. "Is that what you want? Do you want to end up looking like this?" I point at the scars disfiguring my body.

She flinches.

She tries to recover quickly, but not fast enough. I caught the glimpse of fear in her eyes. It should probably hurt my feelings, but I have very little left to feel.

I've learned to choose the people I let into my heart deep enough to cause me pain.

And I'm not letting her in.

Or anyone else.

Chapter 16

Every time we meet, I let Tina use me to soothe her pain.

She tells me it's not about Chi anymore. She tells me she likes me. I don't believe her, and I honestly don't care either way.

She's been coming here every night for weeks. And every time, we tear at each other until our pain finds release. She's taking more and more risks to visit me and it's gonna have to stop. But I'm too selfish to tell her that. The moments I share with her are the only times I don't feel like I'm going insane.

Today has been another long, tedious, morbid day, and she's joined me on the edge of my bed, to attempt casual conversation for once.

"How are you?" she asks.

"Fox put me in a new area," I say.

"Really?"

"Yeah, I'm working in the greenhouse now."

"Do you like it?"

"Yeah, it's awesome." I roll my eyes, and she gives me a glance before kissing my cheek.

"I'm working for some guy named Smith," I add. "He's a real jackass."

"Jake Smith?" she asks.

"Yeah, you know him?"

She nods. "He's not that bad. His attitude is just an act."

I snort with disgust. *Yeah, right!*

"You don't like many people around here, do you?" she asks.

My lips tilt up on one side. "What could have possibly given me away?"

She looks at me and moves closer to stroke my cheek with her thumb before kissing me lightly.

"But you like me?" she asks.

I smile against her lips.

"Possibly," I whisper, flashing a flirty grin. "What do you think?"

She chuckles and her eyes burn right through mine. Her gaze moves while she takes in the muscles outlined by my shirt and then the scarred flesh of my biceps. That's when her smile freezes into sadness. She looks down and grabs my hand to pull it palm-up in her lap, before running her fingertip along my lifeline.

"Stephen, I want more than this." She pauses to look at me. "I'm starting to really like you and—"

"No, nuh uh," I reply quickly.

I have to convince her that she doesn't feel anything for me. I need her to understand it right now. This is her using me, and me using her, and nothing more. It will never be anything else.

"Why won't you let me?" she asks.

"What?"

"Why won't you let me love you?"

"I think it's a little bit early to call this love, Tina," I reply. "Besides, you already know why."

I look down at my scars to get my point across.

If Fox finds out I care about Tina, no matter how slight my feelings, he will take her from me. The horrors he will inflict upon her are more than I can bear to witness.

I can't allow this curse to be put upon her.

I don't want her to end up like me. I don't want her to end up like Willow.

Tina doesn't know about Willow. She doesn't know Willow is the reason why I can't love anyone.

She has already asked me about my past—my life with Chi, my parents, my potential ex-girlfriends—but I didn't answer any of her questions.

I don't talk about the past.

I don't talk about Willow.

Not with Tina.

Not today.

Not with anyone.

Not ever.

Willow is a secret I keep to myself. She's mine and mine only. My memories of her are mine to keep, and I've never shared them with anyone.

No one knows about us.

Not even Chi.

Not even Fox.

And as for my parents and all that, there's no way I'm going down that route with her or anyone—ever.

Tina runs her fingertips over my scars, but I grab her wrist to stop her. "Don't."

"Stephen, what they did to you, it was inhumane. And it wasn't your fault. They did it because you're too good to obey their sadistic orders. Because you have a good heart and—"

"Don't!" I cut her off.

I don't want to hear the speech again. About how beautiful I supposedly am. About how they did this to me because I didn't want to hurt other people.

I know what I am and she needs to accept it, too.

"I've killed people, Tina." I strike where it hurts because she doesn't want to hear it; she doesn't want to see it, she doesn't want to know. She doesn't want to believe what a monster I am. But she doesn't have a choice. Not when it comes to me, she doesn't.

Whatever it is she thinks she's feeling for me, it has to stop. I will tear it out of her until she sees me for what I truly am.

"Not that time. Not that day they burned your skin." She's relentless. "You chose to let them destroy you rather than obey their orders."

"It doesn't matter, Tina." My voice comes out harsh. I want her to stop. Stop trying to make me feel better. "I've killed other people. Innocent people."

I killed Willow. She died because of me.

"You didn't have a choice," she protests. "I had to do horrible things too, Stephen. Do you really think I don't understand? Do you think I don't know?"

No, actually, she doesn't understand. She doesn't know. And I'm not in the mood for a motivational speech today.

"These scars make you human. They make you beautiful," she continues.

"Yeah, keep on telling yourself that," I shoot back.

I push her hand away from my arm and stand up so I can turn my back to her. "I've heard enough for one night. Please, leave. I need time on my own."

"No, I'm not leaving, Stephen."

She's so damn stubborn. The only person I've ever known to be that stubborn is Chi.

I've tried to ward her off like I did him, but she just keeps coming.

I don't want to hurt her, but if that's what it takes, I will.

I don't want her to love me.

I don't want her to care for me.

Her fingers brush my arm before she locks them around my wrist to pull me toward her.

"Stop pushing me away, Stephen. Stop trying to lock me out."

I turn around to look at her, with my gaze as cold as I can make it. "I never let you in to begin with."

Her face contorts with pain, and I regret the words instantly.

I hate seeing her like this.

I want to make up for hurting her feelings, but it's better for her if I don't.

I feign indifference. I'm as closed off as I can possibly get.

"Leave!"

Her dark blue eyes turn freezing cold.

I can't deal with her pain. I can't take it, even if this is for her own good, even if this is me trying to protect her.

"Please," I add softly. "Just go. Please."

"If I leave, I'm not coming back," she warns me.

"It might be better that way," I reply.

I don't mean a word of it.

I don't want her to leave.

I need her.

I want to tell her.

I want to tell her that I wish I could love her the way she deserves to be cared for.

But I will never allow myself to fall for anyone ever again.

I will never put anyone in danger the way I did Willow.

And if I turn her down now, it will be easier for her than if I reject her later.

Despite what she thinks, she doesn't love me. She likes seeing Chi in me.

This thing between us is nothing more than physical longing—a profound need to dull our pain through human touch.

When I'm with Tina, the dissonance in my life doesn't deafen me anymore. It's the only time I don't feel dead anymore. Because she brings me back to life in ways no one else can.

And then I don't think anymore,

I don't ache anymore,

I don't bleed anymore.

But this isn't love.

I know the difference. This doesn't compare to what I felt for Willow. It doesn't even come close.

I turn around and shut her out. She walks to the door, but I don't move. I don't react. I don't say goodbye.

I miss her already.

Despite everything. Despite my best effort to keep her out, Tina has found her way under my skin.

She's the only good thing I have in this place. And she has agreed to be mine in ways even Willow never did.

She opens the door and leaves.

I close my eyes and sigh.

I've screwed up again.

I don't know why I'm doing this. I don't know why I keep sabotaging myself.

Chapter 17

The next day, a guard walks into my cell.

"Follow me, Richards."

"Good morning to you, too."

What do they want from me now?

The guard leads me down the hall, through the yard, into the infirmary. Then he lets me walk in, steps out, and closes the door behind him.

A nurse is standing there, looking at me.

"What's going on?" I ask.

She doesn't answer my question. "Please, lie down. This is just part of the routine."

I do as she says, but when she grabs a syringe from a close-by table, I sit right back up.

"What's that?" I ask, tilting my chin toward the needle in her hand.

"An inoculation," she replies with a casual tone.

"An inoculation against what?" I ask.

She approaches me, but I move out of the way. My feet find their bearings on the ground and I stand up.

I walk backward until I hit the wall. "Don't come any closer," I snarl at her.

She presses a button on the radio attached to her scrubs. "I have a reluctant here."

The door opens and two guards walk in.

"Get back on the cot, Richards," one of them orders.

"Go to hell!"

I'm ready for them; I've trained long enough now. I can take them both down. They circle me from both sides and I go for the weakest one. I lunge forward and slam into him. His lower back hits the cot and he growls in pain. The other guard attacks me from behind, but I turn around just in time to punch him hard in the ribs. He lets out a huff of air and I grab his shoulders, pushing him against the wall where his head hits the concrete.

"Officer Smith, we have a problem here," the nurse calls into her radio. "Yes, someone from your squad. Richards. He refuses to take the vaccination." She waits a few seconds and nods. "All right, thank you, Officer."

The guard comes at me again and punches me in the jaw. The shock stings me out of focus, but I don't let it stop me. I dive for him and knock him to the ground while the other guy grabs my arms and twists them to force me up.

The door opens and Smith walks in.

"What's going on in here?" he asks, his eyes scanning the scene and landing on me. He shakes his head at me and turns to the nurse. "What's the problem with him now?"

"She's not shooting that shit up my arm," I shout at him.

Smith looks at me from the corner of his eye and smiles smugly. "Richards, that 'shit,' as you call it, will save your life. Believe me, you do want the vaccination."

"What is it for?" I ask.

"Confidential," he says with arrogance. "You should have gotten this shot months ago."

The two guards walk to me cautiously and grab my arms. I struggle and hit the cot so hard it moves a few inches.

"Come on, Stephen, just do as you're told," Smith says while leaning against the wall, with his arms crossed over his chest and a self-satisfied smirk on his face. He won't even help the guards restrain me. The effort is beneath him.

"You will learn to comply, Richards. Trust me."

"Fuck off."

His conceited grin widens, and my nostrils twitch with anger as the guards coerce me to lie down. They lock my arms and legs in place with leather ties while Smith watches. The nurse comes to me and plunges the syringe deep into my vein.

Chapter 18

Tina is back. Despite our fight, she's back.

"They're coming," she says upon closing the door behind her.

I rise to my feet, but I don't get any closer. "What do you mean? Who's coming?"

"The Underground. The rebels. They're invading this camp soon."

"I see."

I don't add anything else. I don't know why she's telling me this. I don't see how this concerns me. If a bunch of rebels want to risk their lives to free the prisoners, I don't see why I should care.

It's not like I want to keep the prisoners here.

I'm as shackled to this place as they are.

"You need to get ready. You need to protect yourself."

So, that's what this is about.

This is about Tina being scared. That I might get hurt. That something might happen to me.

I'm touched, really, but I have very little left to fear. And among the small list of things I do fear, death isn't one of them.

"He'll be here too," she adds.

She doesn't need to elaborate. I know whom she's talking about.

Chi.

"He knows your parents are here," she continues, her tone apologetic. "I had to tell him. I told him a little while ago. I couldn't take the sorrow in his eyes anymore."

I sigh with irritation. I told her Chi should stay away from here. I specifically told her never to give him this location.

And now, Chi is coming for our parents.

He's gonna get himself killed, and for what?

"Is he coming for me, too?" I ask.

Tina shakes her head. "He doesn't know you're here. He doesn't know I'm seeing you."

I nod.

"He thinks you've chosen this path," Tina continues. "He thinks you're working as an officer on your own accord."

"I am not an officer," I retort. "Fox would never trust me enough to promote me."

"I know that, but Chi doesn't."

What a fool! What an idiot!

I shake my head.

What kind of a monster does he take me for? To think I'd be participating in this willingly? As if I asked for this.

"Who told him that?" I ask.

"I don't know. I have my suspicions, but I'm not sure who told him that about you. But it wasn't me. I know you didn't want him to come here. I'm sorry I told him about your parents, Stephen, but he's been looking for two years."

"He'll be coming for me if he knows I'm here. If he truly believes I'm working for the government, it won't be pretty, Tina. Those people have persecuted him his whole life."

"I promise you, Stephen, he doesn't know. He's just coming for your parents."

I haven't seen my parents in almost two years.

I work here, where I know they're being held, but I never see them.

Fox doesn't trust me enough to put me in their area.

He thinks I care about them.

He thinks I would help free them.

But now Chi is coming.

I wonder how he would feel if he knew the truth about me.

If he knew the things they did to me.

Tina doesn't know much about my relationship with Chi. And I'm fine with that.

I don't want to explain.

It's too complicated.

Our mutual resentment runs too deep. Its roots are too thick for Chi and I to tear them out now.

Tina lifts her head to look at me, and her face contorts with sorrow.

I don't know what I let transpire that makes her so sad. I usually try my best to guard my feelings from her, but I don't always manage to do so.

She pushes me toward the bed gently and sits astride me. And despite my better judgment, I let her.

She kisses me. And I let her.

I let her take my pain away. Far, far away.

✹✹✹

"Stephen?"

"Yes, Tina," I answer without moving.

I'm lying on my back, with Tina in my arms and her head on my chest. I comb through her silky blond hair. It's so soft and smooth. Almost as soft as her perfect milky white skin against my tanned broken flesh.

"I want to stay here tonight," she says.

I react right away, with fear tearing at me. "No, you can't."

I reiterate this sentence I've uttered so many times before already. Every time, she tries to convince me she should stay. Every time, I force myself to deny her.

I look her in the eye and shake my head. Refusing her request is more painful than I'm willing to show. I'd rather spend the night with her than stay alone drowning in the anguish and constant ache that drive my life.

"Why not? I..." Her gaze searches mine. "I want more than this."

"Tina, if they find you here..." I pause. "I don't even want to think about it. Just imagining it makes me sick. It's too dangerous."

"I don't have to stay the whole night. Just a few more hours."

"What if someone sees you? How would you explain your presence here so late? You're not supposed to be here in the middle of the night, Tina."

"I don't care. And I'm staying. You can't force me out."

She's so stubborn.

"Fine," I relent, with a sigh. "But you need to leave before dawn."

She smiles at me with victory, and I shake my head at her. She's so damn cute.

"You're unbelievable, you know that?"

I won't deny it; I like the idea of her being here tonight. If she stays, she might help me keep the nightmares away. Maybe I can sleep for once without waking up nauseated, sickened by my own existence.

Who am I kidding? I already know that if she stays, we'll hardly sleep at all.

I will take everything she has to offer.

Because that's all we ever do. Because it's the only thing keeping me sane anymore.

My gaze runs all over her body. She's so damn gorgeous. And she has no idea. It's as if no one has ever told her how beautiful she is—inside and out. Tina is smart and kind, and damaged in ways I could never fix. I got to see it all inside her long before we started hooking up. We were both lost when we found each other. And since then, I've let her consume me completely.

She sends me a glance and rests her chin on my collarbone while tracing my scars with her fingertips, her skin warm against mine.

"Let's do it again," she says, a naughty glint shimmering through her eyes. "I want to be on top this time."

"Nuh uh." I shake my head and rub the sudden crease of my brow with the heels of my hands.

"I want to be the one in control for once," she insists.

I stare at the wall. I feel vulnerable and I hate it. I don't wanna feel this way around her, or anyone ever again.

She doesn't understand. She doesn't know what it would take for me to give her that kind of power over me. I shake my head again.

Losing control might take me back to dark places. Dark places I don't want to visit when I'm with her.

She shifts around and sits on top of me, her legs apart to straddle my thighs.

"Tina, don't," I warn her, but she shushes me with her fingers against my lips.

"Why do you always have to be in control, Stephen?"

Because that's the only way I feel safe.

She moves and presses against me once, twice. I can't think straight. My fingers dig into the flesh of her waist and she smiles down at me. She knows she has won this round like she does every single time. I'm never gonna say no.

"You need to loosen up, Stephen. You're always so wired. You need to relax."

I inhale deeply. She doesn't understand. I can't let go and *just relax*. Not when she wants me to give up control like this. But I'm willing to try.

I will try.

For her.

Chapter 19

I'm sitting on Chi's bed *while we play a game of checkers. I'm winning. I always win. I grin at him as I take down his last piece.*

"You cheated," he shouts right away.

"Nuh uh, I won fair and square," I reply. "T'es qu'un mauvais perdant." You're just a sour loser.

"C'est pas vrai!" That's not true!

His mouth turns into a pout.

Mom's face appears through the crack between the door and the wall. "I have some errands to run. You two remember the rules, right?"

Chi and I have learned all the rules by heart. Chi, especially. Since we moved from home a few months ago, he's been scared the officers might find him.

"Yes, Mom," I reply obediently. "Don't go outside and don't answer the door."

She nods and narrows her eyes. She's always looking at me like that. Like I did something wrong. I blink. I don't know what I did wrong again today.

She leaves without another word. And when she closes the door behind her, I notice a lock on the frame. I stand up, walk closer, and look at it for a while.

"Chi, what's that?" I ask.

"It's a lock," he replies.

"Duh, I know that, genius. Why do you have a lock?"

"Mom put it there," he replies with a shrug.

I let my fingers run over it.

I want one.

I want one, too.

I want a bolt for my door.

"Why did she put a lock on your door?" I ask.

"She said it would keep the monsters away. She said the monsters can't enter my room and snatch me if I keep my door locked."

I stop breathing.

Why would Mom get a lock for Chi, but not me?

Probably because I'm a big boy.

After all, Chi's had lots of nightmares since we moved here. He's always scared. And he cries a lot.

But I'm scared, too.

And I want a lock too, to keep the monsters away—to keep the one and only monster away. Away from me.

Chi shifts behind me, and when his hand connects with my skin, I push him back violently.

"DON'T TOUCH ME!" I shout in his face.

The small of his back hits the frame of the bed, hard, and he lets out a yelp of pain.

Then he blinks at me. Over and over again. Completely stunned.

His eyes well up.

I want to apologize. I didn't mean to react like that. It's just...I was thinking about Dad and...And Chi touched me just then...And...

"I..." I say and pause.

Chi is still blinking, but his face has turned angry. He's mad at me. He's always mad at me.

"I'm sorry," I say. I raise my hands like white flags, but he takes a step back. His mouth has turned into a pout of grief and anger. And a deep scowl has formed on his face.

"Get out of my room!" he shouts.

"I'm sorry," I repeat. But he's not listening.

He pushes me toward the door and I stumble.

"GET OUT!" he yells, the tears in his eyes rolling down his face.

I hurt him. I've hurt him again.

I'm always hurting Chi.

I don't mean to. It just happens. And he doesn't understand.

I open the door and walk away. There's no use arguing with him when he's like this. His heavy sobs echo behind me and my heart squeezes, hard.

I go downstairs. I'm gonna wait for Mom. In our living room. Where it's safe. Safer than my room. I'm gonna wait and ask her for a bolt for my door, too. Surely she'll say yes.

***

Mom takes a while to come back, *and when she's finally here, I run to her. I follow her into the kitchen and I'm smiling because I've found a solution. I will get a lock. A lock for my door. And then the monster can't come in anymore.*

"Mom?" I ask.

Her back stiffens. I always trigger those reactions in her. It didn't use to be that way. When I was very little, Mommy was always sweet and gentle. But one day, something changed and then she stopped being nice to me. Just me, though. I must have done something wrong that made Mom hate me, because she's still nice to Chi. I wanna know what I did wrong, but I'm too afraid to ask.

"Yes, Stephen?" she replies while putting the food away.

"Can I get a lock for my door?" I ask.

Her back tenses up again. She turns around to look at me, and her eyes pin me down as she stands tall over me.

"And why should you get a lock?" she asks harshly.

"I want a lock like Chi's for my room, to keep the monsters out."

I don't tell Mom about the real monster. I don't tell her about Dad. He made me promise not to tell anyone. He said that if I told anyone, the officers would come for Chi and they would do to him what Dad does to me at night.

"You don't need a lock for your room, Stephen," she replies with venom.

"But Chi has one," I reply.

116

"Chi isn't trying to destroy my marriage," she hisses at me.

I take a step back. I don't understand.

"Mom. What...?"

What does she mean?

She locks her eyes on mine and bends over so her face is only inches away. She narrows her eyes at me with deep hatred—hatred for me.

"Do you really think I don't know? That I haven't noticed the little games you play with Daddy at night?" she asks in a cruel voice.

My heart races inside my chest. I swallow hard.

Mom knows.

She knows.

I don't want Dad to know that Mommy knows.

Because if he ever finds out that she knows, he will call the officers. And they'll come to take Chi away. They will take my brother away from me.

I blink.

I open my mouth to speak.

I don't understand what Mom is talking about. What games is she referring to?

Those aren't games. I don't like it when Daddy comes to my room.

"Mom?" I ask.

I want to cry. I don't understand.

She cuts me off. "LA FERME, STEPHEN!" she shouts in my face. SHUT UP, STEPHEN! "Tu m'entends, sale petite *ordure? Ferme-la! J'veux pas t'entendre. Monte dans ta chambre et fous-moi la paix!"* Do you hear me, you little scumbag? Shut your mouth. I don't want to hear about it. Go to your room and leave me the hell alone!

I take a step back. I almost stumble over. I grab the side of the table to hold myself up.

"Do you like it?" she asks. "Do you enjoy stealing Daddy's heart from your own mother?"

I don't understand. Why is Mom saying all these horrible, painful things? Is it really my fault? I did ask Daddy to stop. Many times. I asked him to stop.

"You are nothing but a nasty little twerp. You stole my husband and now you want a lock for your door? You've made your bed, Stephen. Now lie in it."

I take another step back, and another, and another. Mommy's words...Mommy's words are like knives cutting through me. They hurt me so badly. They hurt me as much as Daddy.

I take another step back and run out the door. I leave the house and run, and run, and run.

I hide in the woods. They can't find me. Right here in the woods, the monsters can't catch me.

Chapter 20

Stephen - Nineteen Years Old

Tina woke up and left while I was still sleeping, long before the guard comes to my cell.

Fox wants me in his office. That's the first time he's ever called me there. Stuck between two guards, I drag my carcass through the halls and up the stairs.

I enter the room and the luxury of the place sickens me.

A leather couch sits on an Oriental rug, facing a mahogany desk so wide it takes most of the space. A matching leather armchair is positioned behind the desk.

I walk in and wait for Fox's arrival while a guard keeps watch by the door.

I take in the library, where leather-bound books fill the shelves. Classic books. I grab one and peruse through it. The smell of old, dusty paper reaches my nose and I inhale deeply.

I haven't read a book in two years. Reading is one of those things they took from my life. One of those things that I miss.

"I didn't take you for a literature lover, Stephen." His voice echoes behind me, and I put the book back on the shelf.

"I didn't take you for one to enjoy such refinement either," I reply with a defiant grin.

Of course, Fox is a highly educated man. He has the power, the money, and the resources for it. I just have a hard time believing he'd have the soul to enjoy the subtlety of Keats's poetry or to feel the pain of someone like Baudelaire.

He smiles at me despite my impertinence.

I don't like the smug look on his face.

He knows something that I don't.

Something that brings him pleasure.

Something that will hurt me.

"I'm afraid I've come bearing bad news, Stephen."

I try my best not to react.

Does he have another test for me?

I've been here for two years. I thought we were past that stage.

Or it's something else.

He knows! He knows the rebels are coming and he's trying to gauge if I know anything...or whether I'd help my brother.

"I'm afraid your mother just passed away."

The words slap me in the face, and I almost stumble from the blow. "What?"

"Your mother fell sick with pneumonia. She passed away last night," he says, his cold voice empty of all humanity. "I'm sorry for not telling you she was sick. There was nothing we could do, really."

A deep stab of sorrow cuts through my heart.

And then numbness.

And pain again.

Mother just passed away.

I don't know why I feel sad about this.

I don't know how I'm supposed to react exactly.

I'm lost.

I should probably be relieved. Or happy maybe?

But a sense of loss overtakes me instead, my whole life disappearing under my feet, my past evaporating while the pain Mother put me through resounds inside me more deeply than ever.

So much time wasted suffering, for what?

"I'm sorry for your loss," he says, and I could punch him in the face.

He's not sorry at all.

He doesn't add another word. He beckons for the guard to take me away. Then he heads to the window, turning his back to me, and looks at this camp of death he's so proud of.

And despite how I felt about Mother, I add her death to the list.

The list of things I will make Fox pay for eventually.

Chapter 21

The rebels are here. Chi is here with them. Just like Tina said he would be. She hasn't come to my cell in over a week, but she was right about my brother. I hadn't seen him in two years, but he's here walking toward me right now.

"I'll be damned! My little brother, right here in our camp! Tsk, tsk!" I taunt him as I look at him. *How did he get all those bruises?* "What the hell happened to your face, Chi?"

He responds instantly, with his gun pointed at me.

My own brother.

My own blood.

His first reaction upon seeing me after two years is to point his freaking gun at me.

His expression alone could rip my heart out. His hatred for me flows through his veins like the blood we share.

I have this sudden urge to hurt him. So much so that I can hardly control myself.

I want to hurt him, hurt him so badly he will never stand again.

"So, tell me, Brother, what are you doing here? Looking for our parents, I presume."

"Don't call me that. I am not your brother and they are not your parents," Chi shoots back at me.

I could break him right now. After everything I did for him, he came for our parents, but he would let me rot in this hellhole.

"Well, legally, they are my parents more than they are yours. See, according to the law, I am the only child they have. And you, you're just non-existent. I could kill you right here and it'd be like you never were."

"You are a traitor and a coward! I don't care what the law says, Stephen. You stopped being their son the moment you betrayed them."

Did he just call me a coward?

"Do you know what it's been like for me all those years?" I snap at him. "Having to lie through my teeth every moment of my life. Starving to death every second of each day."

Of course, he doesn't know. Because he's a fool. *A blind, ignorant fool!*

"Stop whining, Stephen, it's pathetic," Chi hisses back at me. "You're pathetic!"

His words cut me deep and I retaliate. I will break him before he breaks me.

"Mother and Father deserved what they got, Chi, and in good time, so will you."

The idiot raises his gun higher, right at my forehead.

Fool! I've been training for two years. I could take him down before he even got the chance to blink.

"Tsk tsk! What're you gonna do, Baby Brother? Blow my head off?" I laugh in his face. "I'll react before you can even pull that trigger. So you're going to listen to me and follow me nicely."

"I'd rather die."

"Your choice!" I aim higher.

Come on, Baby Brother, pull that damn trigger and take me down. I know you want to.

The girl with the curly, black hair screams and I turn toward her. Chi's girlfriend, I presume. The one Tina told me about. Chi doesn't deserve her.

"Well, well, well. Look what we got here. Looks like Little Brother got himself a new girlfriend."

Chi blanches right away. He tries to recover quickly, but it's too late. I know him too well.

"She's not my girlfriend. She's just a member of the group."

Nice try! What kind of a moron does he take me for?

"Oh really?" I point the gun at her to see if he'll react. "You won't mind if I shoot her, then. What do you say? I'll give you a choice—it can be you or it can be her."

Even then, he still doesn't shoot. He doesn't have the balls to kill me, even to save his girlfriend's life. *Pathetic!*

"So, Brother, which one is it?" I challenge him.

"I'm not gonna play your little games. Whatever I say, you'll shoot us both anyway. I'm your twin brother, remember. I know what you're thinking and I know how you're thinking."

No matter what I do, no matter what I say, Chi won't kill me. Disappointment flows through me, soon followed by hope. *Maybe he does care about me after all.*

Don't fool yourself, he's just too much of a weakling to take you down. You mean nothing to him!

Right!

"Fine, it'll be her first then. I want you to watch." I press the tip of my gun harder against her forehead, but Chi still doesn't react. "I will shoot her, Brother. I will kill her, just like I did Willow!"

Chi freezes. He freezes and looks at me, blinking like he used to do when we were little and I would say something he couldn't quite digest.

"What did you just say?" he asks.

His hands are shaking. He's almost there. Maybe if I push him again, just a little bit more.

"Are you deaf now, Little Brother?" I laugh in his face, though joy is the last thing I'm feeling right now. Talking about her cuts like a dagger, and I can hardly stand under the pain.

But I push him a bit more.

Closer, closer. Closer to the edge.

"I... will... kill... her... just.... like... I... did... Willow."

I push him again, but my voice breaks. I haven't said her name in two years. Not once since she died.

"It was you?" He's looking at me like I'm the monster he's always believed me to be.

"Well, of course! Who did you think it was?" I taunt him. *Fool!* "Obviously, you didn't get the brains in our family, Chi, if you haven't figured it out yet!" He's a moron if he thinks I'd ever lay a finger on Willow.

"When the authorities took Mother, Father, and me away, I had to prove my loyalty to the officers. It was either that or get tortured. And I cared more about myself than I did you, so when they asked for your location, I just gave it away."

His face contorts with disdain. Not once does he question my words. I could just kill him. I hate him. I hate him for everything I went through. For everything they did to me. For not giving a shit about me. *I fucking hate him!*

"I truly thought Mother had sent you to stay with Willow's family," I say. "I was hoping that once the officers found you, they would drag you here, or even better, maybe kill you. But I guess Mother didn't trust me enough to share any real information with me. That really hurt my feelings, you know, to realize that Mother lied to me like that."

Chi is too blinded by hatred to tell the truth from my lies. He simply accepts all this shit I'm throwing at him as simple facts. It almost hurts my feelings.

Almost.

He's my brother. My twin. But he's never known me at all.

126

I look at him with spite. *Biased, ignorant fool!* I will break him. He won't walk out of here unscathed. I will scar him the same way the officers did me.

"So, tell me, Brother. Where have you been all this time? Ever cared to look for me? Ever wondered how I was doing?" I ask because the foolish part of me is hoping he might still care just a little bit.

"Why would I worry about you?" he asks. "You've been doing perfectly fine."

I tighten my fists. I want to make him crawl on his knees. My whole body is wrecked, covered in scars because I tried to protect his sorry ass. And this is how he thanks me for it.

"What about Lila?" Chi now yells in my face. "She was your girlfriend!"

"Yeah, some poor pathetic girl passed on to me. Did you ever really look at her? Damn, that girl was ghastly! So I should have put up with the ugly duckling while you would get sweet, beautiful Willow. I don't think so!"

I don't believe a word of this crap I'm spewing at him. Lila was a good person. I liked her. But she wasn't Willow. No one will ever compare to Willow.

And Chi is starting to piss me off. Seriously piss me off.

"And to think that Mother and Father were supposed to stand up for what's right in society," I say. "Claiming to want freedom and equality for all. Right! They didn't hesitate to push that hideous chick on me and rip my heart right out of my chest!"

"You were never forced to date her and you know that."

Idiot! What a fucking idiot! Even when I tell him the truth right to his face, he still doesn't get it. He will *never* believe me.

"Yeah, whatever. You're nothing but a blind fool, Chi."

I've had enough. Time to change the game. I look at his girlfriend instead. She looks so innocent, with her big, dark eyes shifting between the two of us.

She's more than Chi deserves, really.

"Chi did tell you about her, right? Our sweet, beautiful Willow. Did he tell you about their first night together too?"

Her mouth drops open in shock.

She didn't know.

Of course she didn't. Chi is a born liar. His birth was a lie. His childhood was a lie. Everything about him is a lie.

"Shut up!" he barks at me, and I smirk in his face.

"Oh, he didn't tell you?" I sneer and force the knife in deeper. "He told me all about it, you know. I had to listen to him brag about how they did it in the barn behind her house and how soft her skin was."

Her eyes well up and she blinks fast. He never told her about Willow.

I shake my head. Tsk, tsk, tsk.

Little Brother and his many, many secrets.

This poor innocent girl doesn't know the first thing about him.

"Oh, he didn't tell you?"

I laugh.

128

Not at her.

At him.

His hands tighten around his gun, but he still doesn't shoot.

"You need to realize that Chi has spent his whole life living a lie. All he knows is deception. You'll never be able to trust him."

"Don't listen to him, Thia! He's a psychopath! He's just trying to mess with our heads. He's getting at me through you."

I snort at that, but I'm suddenly really tired. Tired of being here. Tired of dragging my carcass around this place. Tired of living. *Living for what, anyway?*

"This is getting tedious and I have a camp to guard. I'll just get along with this. Chi doesn't seem to think you matter enough for him to step up for you," I tell her, "so I'll just have to shoot you both, I guess."

I smile just a bit. Even then Chi doesn't do a thing to take me down. *Wimp!* I can't believe we came from the same womb.

I'm gonna have to stab deeper. This is getting truly exhausting. "By the way, Chi, just so you know, there was no need to look for Mother. She passed away last week. As always, Little Brother, it looks like you made it just a little bit too late."

The agony on Chi's face doesn't even make me feel good. It's just painful to watch, really. *Who would have thought that after all this time I would still feel any compassion for him?*

"I don't believe you!"

His voice shakes under the weight of his words. He's aching. And I stab again, just one last time, really, really deeply. He never cared about me, but he's always loved her so much—our sick, sick Mother.

"Aww, but she did! She got pneumonia. You know how it is these days. They didn't really care to cure her. I would have helped, but I'm pretty busy, you know."

"I'm going to kill you, right here, you miserable piece of shit!"

He says it but does nothing. Empty promises. As always.

"Oh, no need for name calling, Brother."

And suddenly the sirens blow around the camp and gunshots echo around the yard.

Chi knocks the rifle out of my hands and grabs my wrist. Little Brother is finally gonna kick my ass. And I will let him. Because I am so tired of fighting back.

"Thia, the gun!" he calls to his girlfriend.

But she doesn't react.

And then *he* shows up—the monster in my life.

Father.

He appears like a ghoul out of nowhere.

I can't breathe. Terror grabs me by the throat. I can't breathe.

I pat around blindly for my gun. *Where's my gun?*

I try to breathe.

Father takes another step forward.

I can't breathe.

I'm lying defenseless on the ground.

Where's my gun, damn it?

Father can't hurt me.

I won't let him hurt me again.

He can't hurt me.

He can't hurt me here.

There are people around us. He can't hurt me.

I can't breathe.

"Dad?" Chi asks. And the love he feels for our father cuts through his voice to slash at my heart like a blade.

"Chi, my son, you've come for me!"

Father takes a step toward Chi.

He's not getting out. Not if I can help it. He'll walk out of here when I'm dead.

I'm not letting him out, free to go as he pleases, to hurt other kids the way he almost destroyed me.

I head-butt Chi in the nose, and he loosens his grip on me. I find my weapon at last, grab it, and roll on the ground.

I shoot, once, twice.

Father falls and relief flows through veins, releasing my heart from its heavy weight.

He will never hurt me again.

I am floating.

I am free.

I am finally free.

Father will never hurt *anyone* ever again.

Chi pins me down.

Wrath overtakes him and he pummels me for good. He hits me with his fist, and this time, he doesn't stop.

An image rolls in front of my eyes repeatedly: Father falling, falling, falling to the ground.

His blood is on my hands. His blood is inside my head.

I want it out!

I can't breathe.

His image won't go away.

Rolling, rolling inside my head.

Make it go away!

What have you done?

Father has won and I have lost—everything.

What have you done?

I never wanted his blood on my hands.

What have you done?

He's inside my head.

I want him out!

The sobs rise to choke me as I silently beg for Chi to finally kill me. To please, please, please, free me. To put me out of my misery. But the words won't come out. I can't breathe. I'm choking on sobs so strong they're rocking my entire body.

And Chi just keeps on coming, his knuckles meeting my face—this everlasting fight between us finally coming to an end.

And I let him.

132

I don't fight back.

I want to die.

Please, free me.

I let him punch the life out of me.

Stars dance in front of my eyes.

My life finally slipping away.

Chi grabs his gun and hits me, hard.

And everything turns dark.

Chapter 22

Chi and I are in the kitchen with Mother. *The two of them are setting the table while talking about Emile Zola and the books he wrote about the living conditions of the lower class in nineteenth-century France. They're speaking in French and I'm wondering why Mother has spent so much time teaching us a language we'll never use. She claims it's a tradition in our family. I don't believe her. She never does anything without an ulterior motive. I just haven't figured out what her goal is yet.*

Chi pulls me into the conversation. He always wants my opinion on everything. I never talk much. I only use my words to hurt him while hoping he'll finally leave me alone and stop prying into my life.

Looking at him is enough to make me sick. I'm sure he spends a lot of time with Willow. I wonder if she still loves me or if she has fallen in love with him instead. I wonder if he has stolen her heart from me the same way he did Mother's. I wonder how much more he will take away from me.

I have nothing left, nothing I care about.

I'd let go of life altogether, but I won't give my parents that pleasure.

"What do you think, Stephen? Was their situation better or worse than it is here today?" Chi asks.

I give him a quick glance, and vomit rises in my throat. I can't focus on his damn question. All I can think about is him. Him with Willow. And Willow with him. And them having sex.

"Stephen, qu'est-ce que tu penses?" he asks again. What do you think, Stephen?

I don't reply.

"Stephen, answer the question." *Mother casts me a sharp glance.*

"I don't owe him or you an answer," *I shoot back.*

Chi's eyes turn sorrowful and my heart aches.

"How are things going with Willow, dear?" *Mother asks Chi while staring at me.*

My jaw clenches against my will.

"What are you two doing tomorrow?" *she continues, waiting for me to react to her provocation.*

I don't.

I stand still and try my best not to give her the satisfaction. I won't let her see me break down again. She already walked all over my pride when I begged and pleaded with her not to go through with Chi's engagement to Willow. I won't let her see me hurt.

Chi averts his eyes and looks at the floor, his lips rising in a tiny smile.

I hate him!

I can't process what he did with Willow. I can't deal with it.

I'm still aching, hurting, agonizing.

That she agreed to sleep with him, it hurts me so damn much.

It's been killing me slowly ever since Chi came to me, bragging about it like some proud asshole.

The thought of them doing it keeps tearing me apart every second of each day. Every day I wonder if he's with her when I'm at school. I spend all day trying to ignore the thoughts. The thoughts of him touching her. Of him ravishing her.

I try not to think about it.

It's all I can think about.

And his smile right now tells me it has happened against since then—more than once.

I grind my teeth.

I close my eyes.

I try to breathe.

I try not to react.

I try not to start a fight.

I try my best not to punch him in his stupid face.

I don't think I can spend a lifetime going through this torture. It's time I told him. I should take her back—if she still wants me. She was never his to begin with. She was always mine. Never his.

I wonder if she likes it when he touches her.

My teeth clench harder.

Chi raises his eyes to meet Mother's gaze. "Willow wants us to spend some time in the barn, to take care of her chickens."

Liar.

I want to scream at him so badly. What a damned liar he is!

"Yes, those eggs are really good. Please, thank the Jenisons for me," Mother replies, oblivious to the truth. She has no clue what's going on in that barn. What Chi and Willow really do when they meet there.

I hate him!

I ball my hands into fists, ready to punch a hole in the wall.

"What about you and Lila?" Mother asks me, her eyes shining wickedly. She's laughing at my expense. She knows I'm upset and she's enjoying it.

"I told you I wasn't dating that girl!" I reply sharply.

I don't want Mother to see how much I'm hurting. But it's too late for that now. Too late to pretend I don't care.

She snorts at me and pushes the dagger in deeper. "Stephen, I only want what's good for you."

She doesn't mean a word of it. She's pretending for Chi's sake. I'm not as good at acting as she is. I can't pretend I'm okay when she keeps driving knives into my soul. Chi doesn't see these wounds she keeps inflicting upon me. He only sees me react to them, always negatively, always aggressively. She taunts me in ways he doesn't understand.

He can't see her little games for what they truly are—arrows shot by Mother, aimed straight at my heart.

Her fake smile never falters. "I'm sure Lila will grow on you, dear, just like Willow grew on Chi."

Her smile widens and I could scratch it off her face.

"Va au diable!" Go to Hell! I snap at her and slam the door on my way out.

I've screwed up again. Now Mother is gonna cry to appeal to Chi's softer side, to make me look like the bad seed she claims that I am. A nefarious weed she can't quite rip out. A weed sprouting, growing, feeding off the soil of her life.

And every day, hatred spreads through my veins a little bit more. Tightening around my lungs until I'm suffocated by it.

I can't breathe.

I leave the house and go straight to our meeting place. I know quite well Willow won't be there.

Not today. Not any day.

Willow won't be there.

The place will be empty like my carcass of a body.

I drag myself there slowly. I look up and suddenly she's here. Willow is standing right there, waiting for me.

Chapter 23

Stephen - Nineteen Years Old

The rebels came. The rebels left.

Willow is here whispering to me.

She's telling me she loves me.

She's telling me everything is going to be fine.

She's telling me she is still mine and I am still hers.

She's telling me I still have some good left in me.

She's lying.

Her image slowly fades away as darkness squeezes my heart and I turn cold.

My heart is cold.

My heart is ice.

You finally did it. You finally got rid of him.

The voices wake me from my dream and I sit up.

I take in my surroundings.

I'm in my cell.

I'm reliving this nightmare over and over again.

Every day, I just can't seem to wake up from this awful reality.

You did it. He's gone, gone, gone. You shot him at last. He's gone and you are finally free.

My heart races. I shut down my thoughts. I don't want to remember. I don't want to think about him.

I don't want to think about Father.

About what I did.

It's too painful.

My head is pounding. I'm going to throw up.

I stand up and waver as I make my way to the bathroom. I hold myself to the wall before emptying my stomach in the toilet bowl. The sharp pain hammering through my skull forces me to tighten my eyes shut and shake my head to get rid of the dizziness.

Bile rises in my throat again, and I reach for the toilet.

When I'm done, I sit down, with my back against the wall and my knees bent against my chest. I wrap my arms around them, close my eyes, and try to breathe.

An image of Father falling to the ground rolls over and over again inside my aching skull.

I try to block it out.

I try to deny it.

But I can't.

My heart squeezes and a single tear rolls down my cheek.

You're gonna feel sorry for him, now? You're pathetic.

I try to push Father out, out, out.

But he won't leave me be. He's always here, haunting me, taunting me.

I stand up and blink against the blinding luminosity when I turn on the light. Then I rinse my mouth and enter the shower before running the water as cold as it gets.

Father has managed to find his way into my skull. And now he will never leave.

My tears mix with the water dropping down my face as the sobs rise from my chest to choke me.

You're a killer. You're a pathetic, pathetic, pathetic killer.

Slowly, anger and resentment fill my heart and find their usual place inside my useless organ. They flow and overflow. I think about Chi and the look on his face when he saw me.

It was pure bad luck that I walked into him.

All this time, I've tried to protect him.

All this time.

He came to free our parents and his first reaction upon seeing me was to pull a gun at my face.

My own brother.

My own blood.

There are days when I hate him so much I can't breathe.

I don't know when it got to that point.

I don't know how I got here, from wanting to protect him to wanting to see him squirm.

And yet, he still didn't have the guts to pull that trigger. He's too good, too gentle to kill me. But he won't forgive what I did to Father. He won't forgive the lies about Mother either. If we ever cross paths again, he'll try to take me down for good.

And I will welcome it.

I'm craving it.

Chapter 24

Fox has called all the guards to the main yard. He spread terror and carnage all around this place last night.

The rebels came.

The rebels freed some of our prisoners.

The rebels failed to free them all.

When the rebels left, Fox spread hell all over.

While I was out cold.

After Chi beat me up so hard I passed out.

Fox told his guards to shoot every prisoner left in this camp.

Why the hell would he kill his own workers, I have no idea. I've long stopped trying to understand his twisted mind.

Now he's called all of us to clean up his mess.

My stomach curls. I'm having enough trouble keeping my food down on a regular basis. And now corpses upon corpses are piled up along the walls. The guards barrel the bodies away to be incinerated. The air is putrid with decay and I wanna puke. The mere thought of touching the corpses makes me want to hurl. Fox hasn't told us why all the prisoners had to die, and my coworkers just followed the orders without questioning anything.

I've moved past my general apathy, somehow.

I am back to being pure hatred.

I am wrath.

I am all revenge.

Out of all of them, Fox is the one I despise the most.

He took the most precious person in the world to me.

I returned his courtesy in kind. I took his son in return.

I didn't mean for it to happen. It wasn't planned.

Just poetic justice, really.

I was going for the girl when Fox's son jumped in front of her. She was aiming her gun at me, ready to shoot. She left me no other choice. Why the hell would Fox's son risk his life for hers, I have no idea. Probably some idiotic move. I don't care either way.

I could lie. I could say I feel sorry for shooting William Fox.

But I don't.

I don't feel anything.

I am no longer human.

I am a monster.

This monster they've turned me into.

Fox doesn't know.

He doesn't know I'm the one who shot his son.

Willow was an angel, pure and delicate, sent to this world to spread kindness and compassion.

Fox's son was a demon, a monstrosity launched upon the world to destroy it.

I've seen the things he was capable of.

I've seen him join his father while he was torturing people.

I've seen William Fox smile and laugh while his dad was doing it, too.

It might not excuse what I did.

But at this point, I simply do not care.

My hatred for Fox and his family has reached its highest threshold yet, to the point of no return.

I brace myself for what I have to do today. I get ready to clean the horrors that man has forced upon these poor people. And my heart hardens a little bit more than it already did before.

Chapter 25

I'm dreaming. I must be dreaming because Willow is here. I stir around and open my eyes. I'm in my cell, back from spending yet another day in hell.

I was dreaming. I had finally reached heaven. I close my eyes to recapture the illusion, a sweet memory from when Willow and I were sixteen years old.

I close my eyes and let the dream submerge me. I'm floating and all the pain starts fading away.

She's here.

She's here at last.

I am alive.

I am breathing.

I am at peace.

I am in love.

We're sitting under a tree in the woods close to her house. I hold her hand and listen to the birds singing. Willow can recognize most of the sounds and point out the names of the birds, their colors, their peculiarities.

She fascinates me.

I turn around and marvel at her while she speaks. Her voice is soft, caressing and peaceful.

She turns to me too, and I drown.

In her deep turquoise blue eyes.

I drown.

I have nothing to hold on to. I just let go.

"What did you learn today, Stevie?"

She asks me this every day. And every day, I reply the same thing.

But not today.

Today, I have something else to say.

Something I've been meaning to tell her for a while, but never gathered the courage to.

I look her in the eyes, her deep blue eyes, and let the water flow everywhere and all around me.

I let myself drown as I caress her cheek with my thumb and stroke her skin, so soft I could die.

I take a breath, lean toward her, and kiss her as tenderly as I possibly can. She is porcelain, she is fragile. I'm trying my best not to break her.

I make my way to her ear, depositing kisses along her jaw line, and she giggles. The bells from heaven resonate in my ears and I'm finally at peace.

I kiss her earlobe and whisper sweet words to her.

"Je t'aime, mon amour."

She giggles. "What does it mean?"

"For me to know and you to find out." I smile at her and she giggles some more.

I pull her face to mine and press my lips against hers.

And I must be dead for sure because everything is peace and sweetness.

Willow is beauty.

She is kindness.

She is more than I deserve.

"I love you," I whisper against her lips.

I kiss her like I never did before, and she lets me.

She pulls away just slightly, with innocence and benevolence sparkling through her eyes. "I love you too, Stevie."

My heart races.

It takes flight.

It springs its wings and leaves my chest.

I die and am reborn in one second.

In the one second it took for her to say the words.

Words I was hoping for.

Words I was waiting for.

Words to free me from my chains.

Words to quiet the voices inside my head.

Words to slay my demons.

I beam at her and caress her jaw with my lips, following the sweet, tender path leading from her mouth to her ear.

She giggles once more. "Stevie?"

"Yes, sweetheart?" I exhale against her skin.

"Do you think it's possible? For us to be together forever?"

She says it and my heart aches. The only way for us to be together like that would be to run away.

148

I don't want her anywhere near my family.

I don't want them to spoil her soul.

I don't want them to tarnish her purity.

"Yes, sweetheart. We will be together forever. Just you and me, forever."

My heart aches. I'm lying.

I'm lying because she needs me to say it.

Because I need to believe it.

Because I'm craving it.

I've never wanted anything more in my life. I've never wanted anything as much as I want to be with her, spend time with her, and love her.

She deserves better. You are no good. No good. No good for her.

I push the voices away and brush her lips with mine again, teasing her mouth open with the tip of my tongue. Our kiss deepens.

She's all I've ever wanted.

I pull back and whisper in her ear, "What are you hiding behind your back, sweetheart?"

She giggles. "Nothing."

I kiss her earlobe and she shivers against me.

"Really? So you won't mind if I look?"

Before she can reply, my arm wraps around her body and I reach for the thing she's holding in her hand. I pull it toward me before she can protest.

"You're not supposed to look at it now," she says.

"Why not now?" I smile at her innocently, knowing quite well she can never resist me when I play the flirting card.

"I wanted you to look at it when you're home."

I am home. You are home.

"Can I open it now, please?" I kiss her cheek.

She can never say no to me. I know that and beam at her while batting my lashes as I repeat, "Please."

She laughs and nods. Her entire face has turned red, a rose opening under my touch as I kiss the curve of her jaw and whisper, "Thank you."

I pull away and stare at the package in my hands. It's flat, rectangular, and covered in wrapping paper. I tear the paper off, slowly. I don't want to damage whatever she put inside. And when the wrap comes off and lands on the ground, a picture of Willow appears and stares back at me from the surface of a sheet of paper.

I throw a glance at Willow, who is hiding behind her hands as if she's ashamed.

"It's beautiful. Why are you hiding?"

She bites her lower lip when I pull her hands away from her face.

"I didn't want to see your reaction."

I smile at her. "This is the most beautiful gift anyone has ever given me."

I look at the picture Willow drew of herself and then I look at her. She stares at me with her big blue eyes and smiles timidly.

"You like it?" she asks.

150

"I love it."

I place the drawing on the leaves next to me and reach her jaw with my hand. I kiss her forehead, her eyelids, her cheeks, her throat, and her mouth. I stroke her tongue delicately while pushing her slowly to the ground. We lie in the leaves, and I try not to crush her as I kiss her more and more deeply. I can never get enough of her.

I kiss her and she tugs at my hair.

But something's wrong.

I kiss her and slowly her image fades away. Away from underneath me.

I reach for her and call her name.

"Willow? Willow, what's happening?"

But the darkness is here. The darkness is here to engulf me.

It's pulling me away from her.

I try to hold on.

The darkness pulls at me and I open my eyes.

Willow is gone.

I'm in a cell.

In my cell.

Imprisoned.

Caged in.

Always and forever.

I close my eyes and try to reach her again, but she's gone—forever.

My cold heart aches.

She has melted the ice inside me during one single dream. And I am now aching.

I try to rebuild the wall.

The wall of ice around me.

But it's too late.

I stir around.

I sit up.

I stand up.

I stumble.

I fall to my knees, with tears rolling down my cheeks.

Sometimes I wish she wouldn't visit me at all.

Her departure is always the worst, the worst sensation I have ever felt.

Ten minutes of her presence are enough to make one second of her absence unbearable.

And I can't, I can't take this pain anymore.

Chapter 26

That evening, Tina walks into my cell.

I hadn't seen her since she talked to me about the rebels coming to our camp. I've missed her, though I'm still trying to get over my dreams from last night. Though I'm still trying to get over spending time with Willow. Though I'm still trying to let go.

"Where have you been?" I ask.

"Sorry I couldn't come here for a while," she replies.

"I was getting worried, Tina. Did Fox keep you busy on the outside or something? It's been crazy out here."

Tina shakes her head sadly. "I was framed."

"What do you mean you were framed?"

I take a couple of steps toward her.

"Someone gave away the location of our liaison and they said I'd done it."

I grimace. I don't understand.

"I would never do that. The only reason why I work as an officer in this godforsaken place is to help the Underground. I'd never give our liaison away. They thought I wanted Chi to get arrested. I would never do that, Stephen."

She's close to tears. Tina hardly ever cries.

I take a few strides toward her and pull her petite frame against mine. I kiss the top of her head. I kiss her hair. I hold on to her shoulders and look her in the eyes.

"What happened?"

"Taylor was furious. He sent some members of the Underground to come for me. They put me in detention. They only do that to traitors. I tried to explain. I tried to convince Taylor I had nothing to do with it."

"He held you captive?" Anger flares inside my chest.

"They kept me prisoner, yes."

I narrow my eyes. "How did you get out? Where did they keep you?"

"The only reason why Taylor didn't kill me is because I've provided valuable information before and he doesn't have the authority to kill a traitor without authorization from the main leader."

"How did you get out?"

Her eyes well up again, and though she still hasn't answered my question, I hold her more tightly against my chest and change the subject. "What did Fox say when you didn't show up for work?"

"I told him my cover was jeopardized. I told him I could re-infiltrate the Underground. I need to be of use here if I still want to be useful to the rebels." She averts her eyes. "Stephen?"

"Yes."

She looks back at me. "When I was away, I had time to think and I was wondering...How come you never asked me?"

"What?"

"How come you've never asked me to help you get out of here? I have the skills. I have the status. I know you hate it here. I know you hate this job and they keep you locked up in this camp like an animal. Why didn't you ask me to help you leave? If Fox won't let you out, I could help you escape."

I frown. "I have nowhere to go. I don't deserve freedom."

A small gasp escapes her mouth, so light I'm not sure it was really there. "Stephen, you don't deserve this. Whatever you may have done, you don't deserve what they did to you."

Here we are again. With her trying to convince me that I am good.

I hate it when she does that.

I don't want to hear it.

I know what I am. I know what I did.

She strokes my jaw, and I flinch under her touch.

I can't do this anymore.

I glance at her. "I'm glad you're safe now, Tina. But you should leave."

She gives me the look—that excruciating look she uses against me any time I try to push her away.

I keep my gaze on her, forcing myself to face the damage I've done. But she's not sad at all; she seems more determined than ever.

"I've been through a lot these past few days, Stephen. I'm here with you now and I'm not leaving."

She runs her fingertips over my chest, outlining my muscles through my shirt, while her sultry dark blue gaze roams my face.

"Are you sure you want me to leave?" she asks.

Chapter 27

"**Time for lunch,**" Smith yells at the prisoners.

Every shoulder in the greenhouse sags in relief at this short break from such exhausting labor. The inmates form a line in the aisles between the sprouts of vegetables, and they wait for Smith to open the cafeteria door. He slides his pass through the padlock and enters a code. When a short beep echoes through the greenhouse, the door opens and I stand by the line with my gun in my hands. I watch as the female prisoners pass by me, but not one of them looks at me. They all stare at the ground while dragging their feet through the dust. When everyone has made it into the cafeteria, I step inside.

There are about sixty inmates working in this greenhouse, with two guards and one officer surveying the area—Smith being the officer in charge.

The prisoners line up by the counter, where the cook serves them indescribable food of questionable texture and color. Then they proceed to sit in their respective seats at the large tables filling the cafeteria.

Smith, Reynolds, and I tour the tables the entire time. The prisoners don't talk when we're around. They eat, with their noses almost touching their plates, to avoid looking at us.

"What do you mean you're not hungry, huh?" Smith says loud enough for everyone to hear. He's bending over a prisoner's shoulder, with his mouth close to her ear.

"This isn't food," the frail woman replies.

Smith smacks the back of her head and the sound reverberates all the way across the room.

"You will eat or you will starve, you hear me?" he snaps at her.

His hand is raised and he strikes her once more, across the face this time. My hands turn to fists, and I'm running so quickly I reach him before he gets to hit her again.

"That's enough," I hiss as I grab his wrist.

His dark brown eyes turn metallic cold as he shoots me a once-over.

"What the hell do you think you're doing, Richards?" he asks. "You're under my command. Let go of my wrist before I feed you my knuckles."

I release him, but I don't move. I stand in his face, and his eyes turn deadly.

"Step away right this instant," he warns me.

"Or what?"

Smith flashes me a contemptuous smile, and as retaliation for my insubordination, he grabs the prisoner by her hair and pulls her right off the bench. She falls to the ground, and Smith drags her between the tables. She kicks

158

and struggles to stand up, all the while scratching his arms, but he doesn't let go.

"I'll show you submission," he snarls at her for everyone to hear.

The message is clear. He's going to beat her up and probably rape her until she begs for his forgiveness.

I run after them and slam my shoulder into his side. The shock forces his grip off the prisoner and we fall on top of each other right next to her. And then I hit his face and I pummel him to the ground before I can even process what I'm doing. And I can't stop. I've seen this man treat these prisoners like shit too many times already. Enough is enough.

My knuckles meet the flesh covering his cheekbones and the skin of my hands breaks on impact. He hits me in the stomach, but I don't move.

"You're weak," I taunt him. "Is this the best you can do?"

His eyes slit with a thirst for murder and he head butts me in the nose, almost breaking it. I hit him in the face again.

From the corners of my eyes, I see the prisoners rising to their feet, staring at us without moving any further. An alarm suddenly rings in my ears and it takes me a couple of seconds to understand that someone has pulled the siren calling for reinforcement. Soon five officers swarm the cafeteria and come to force me away from Smith. I fight back, but their grip is strong.

"You're dead, Richards," Smith threatens, before rising to his feet and wiping the blood off his split bottom lip. He spits on the ground and stares right at me while pretending to slit his throat with his index finger.

"Don't make promises you can't deliver," I tell him with a languid smile.

His nostrils flare and the officers drag us both out of the cafeteria.

Chapter 28

Fox walks into his office.

He raises his eyes to us with distaste and flicks his hand at the officers without looking at them. The men exit the room, and Fox walks around his desk to sit in the leather chair behind it. He doesn't invite us to take a seat, but I do anyway. Smith, however, remains standing, with his hands behind his back and his head lowered in submission. *Sucker!*

Fox sighs. "What makes you two think I have time for your drama and personal feuds? This isn't preschool. I'm getting tired of your antics."

Smith cowers in front of our boss while I roll my eyes.

"You are a lame example for our prisoners," Fox adds. "Especially you, Smith."

"I was only doing my job, Sir," Smith replies. "Richards—"

"Shut your mouth," Fox snaps at him before cutting me a quick, sharp glance. "I'm used to Richards disobeying the rules, but I was expecting better from you, Smith."

"I...I apologize, Sir." Smith's head is bent so low his chin is almost buried in his throat.

"I'm promoting Stephen to the rank of officer," Fox says without a speck of emotion. "He'll be in charge of the greenhouse from now on, and you will be moved to another area."

"Excuse me?" Smith asks with dismay. "Sir, with all due respect, he's not mature enough to become an officer. He—"

Fox raises his index finger to shut him up.

"I've checked our records over the past few months, Jake," he says, "and I was surprised to see how much productivity our prisoners achieve under Stephen's supervision. His area has been producing slightly more than any other areas in this camp. I've been testing my theory and moving him to different places. First, the apicultural room and now the greenhouse. It could be a coincidence, but I've watched the videos and I've been observing Stephen. He seems to have a certain compassion toward our prisoners that the rest of you lack."

"Sir, we're not supposed to befriend the inmates," Smith replies. "I saw him share food with one of them just a few days ago. That's against the rules—"

Fox shoots Smith a cold, green gaze that cuts him right off.

"Production is the ultimate goal of this camp, Smith. Do you think housing those people comes for free? I don't care how productivity is achieved, I want better results. Stephen will be on trial until I have proof that there is, in fact, a correlation between his attitude toward the prisoners and their productivity."

Great! This so-called reward is a poisoned gift. Fox knows I hate working here. This is just another way for him to mess up with my head.

"I never said I was gonna take that position," I say.

Fox sends me a look and smiles wickedly, like he knows something that I don't. The ice in his eyes shoots a shiver down my spine, and I try hard not to shudder.

He flicks his index finger at Smith and gives a head tilt toward the door. "You can leave now. I will assign you to your new area soon. In the meantime, you are dismissed until further notice."

"Sir, please, I—"

"Just go home, Smith."

Jake grits his teeth and casts me a murderous glare. I give him a smug smile and wriggle my fingers at him.

He mumbles, "Better hope I never catch you alone in a corner, Richards."

I chuckle at his threat. *Am I supposed to be scared? Loser!*

He slams the door on his way out, and Fox moves from his seat to come and stand in front of me. He leans against his desk and grins before his face turns serious again.

"I've lost quite a few guards thanks to the rebels," he starts, "but it didn't take much to hire new people to replace them. I want you to train some of the new guards, the ones who will be working in your area, under your command."

"And what if I refuse?" I ask again.

His lips curl up.

"There are ways to convince you this is in your best interest. I know you wouldn't want to see those you care about getting hurt. Say, Officer Davis, for example."

I try to remain impassive, but fail miserably. My emotions surface against my will, and Fox's scornful grin spreads on his disgusting face.

"Come on now, Stephen. Did you really think I wouldn't notice this thing going on between you two? I have cameras all over this place. I know she's been visiting you, and I know it's more than friendship."

A glint shines through his eyes.

He put a camera in my cell, hidden, that we weren't aware of.

Bile rises in my throat. I swallow it down and try my best to remain silent. He may have spied on us, but it doesn't sound like he's heard what Tina had to say. He doesn't know she's on the rebels' side.

"Do this job for me and Tina will be safe. Refuse to cooperate and I will put her through more misery than even you have faced so far. I think we both know how much you care about her. You may want to think about this carefully and not disappoint me again."

I inhale deeply and nod. *What else am I supposed to do?*

Tina and I weren't careful enough. I have to make sure she doesn't pay for our indiscretions.

"You won't access a gun anywhere outside your work area, and someone else will let you in and out." He smiles at me again. "Fooled me once, won't fool me twice. Right?"

My nostrils twitch.

"So, what do you think, Stephen? Do we have a deal?"

I cast him a quick glance. He's holding all the cards and I'm forced to play by his rules.

"We have a deal," I reply.

What else am I supposed to say?

He rises to his feet and shakes my hand.

Chapter 29

Tina and I broke up.

It's not something I like to think about.

It's all I can think about.

I miss her so damn much. *How could I be so dumb as to let her get under my skin like this?* Her absence cuts me so deeply I can no longer sleep.

She got upset over some friend of hers that I shot when the rebels attacked the camp. Some guy named James. Like I was supposed to know who that guy was to her.

I shot my own father for goodness' sake. *Why should I care about some random dude who meant nothing to me?* He was about to take me down. A pure case of shoot or die.

I guess it's not like Tina and I ever really were together.

It's not like this was a relationship, or like we were really a couple.

But it still hurts me like hell every time I think about her.

I can't sleep. I can't eat.

I haven't seen her since then and it's just as well. I can't forgive her. She's like everybody else in my life. They always claim they love me, but all they want is to use me until they can dispose of me—Father, Mother, Chi, and now Tina.

It's not like I didn't warn her. She refused to see the rotten apple in me. Sin and decay have festered inside my heart for so long. She was foolish to think I could grow into anything good.

I sigh deeply and shake my head.

Footsteps echo on the ground by my side, stirring me from my thoughts as a prisoner comes to stand in my way.

"Officer Richards?" she asks.

"Yes, Joy, what is it?"

The blonde girl stares at me with huge doe eyes, startled that I actually know her name. I never call the prisoners by the numbers printed on their garments or tattooed on their skin.

Joy lowers her head and clears her throat. "I was told to come to you and ask if you might need my services tonight, Sir."

I wrinkle my nose at Joy's salacious offer, and she squirms when she sees the disgust on my face. I never partook in the activities most officers revel in—mainly abusing our inmates and subjecting them to forced prostitution. I'm not mad at Joy, though—just the whole system.

"Who told you to come to me?" I ask.

She looks at me through her eyelashes. "Officer Smith."

My hands turn to fists. *When was he here?* I thought he was guarding some other area.

"When did he ask you to come see me?"

"Yesterday, he told me your broken heart needed mending, so he sent me to see what I could do."

She flushes and averts her eyes. She obviously doesn't want to be here.

How did Smith find out about Tina and me anyway?

I lean toward Joy.

"Joy, I don't want you in my bed tonight. Actually, I don't want you in any officer's bed tonight. I will tell Smith I've accepted your offer, and I'll let him know I've made a claim on you. That means you are mine now and no guard in this area can touch you or there will be consequences."

She won't look at me. Her eyes remain glued to the ground, her cheeks flushed. "Should I join you tonight, then?"

I shake my head and grab her shoulders to force her to look at me. Her gaze flies to me and she blinks back her welling tears.

"No, Joy, you're not joining me or any other guard tonight or any other night. And I'll take care of anyone trying to touch you."

I might be putting her in danger by claiming her as mine. Smith might assault her just to get back at me. I swear I'll break every bone in his face if he lays one finger on her.

The guards under my command fear me too much to try anything against me, though. They're scared of my scars.

Idiots! I used to hide the marks on my skin, until I realized the effect they have on people. I started wearing short sleeves after the rebels attacked the camp, and the newbies look at me like I'm some boogieman. I don't try to persuade them otherwise.

Joy clears her throat. More tears have pooled in her eyes, now streaming down her cheeks in long rivers of relief.

"Officer Richards, how could I possibly repay you?" she asks.

I sigh. "You got here two weeks ago, right?"

She wipes her tears away with the back of her hand and sniffles a few times.

"Yes, Sir, I did."

"How did you end up here?"

She blinks in confusion. "What do you mean?"

"How did you end up in this camp?" I ask.

She blushes profusely and averts her eyes with shame. "I...I lost my virginity to a man who wouldn't marry me. He was not my promised fiancé either. I...I made the mistake of falling for him. It was my fault."

"Your fault?" I ask with disbelief. "How was that your fault?"

Joy stares at me, gauging whether I'm playing games with her or not. "I should have known better. I knew the consequences."

I shake my head at the profound bigotry so skillfully ingrained into this girl's mind.

"So, you think you are where you belong, then?" I ask, raising an eyebrow. "That you deserve to be here?"

She looks at the ground again and doesn't reply.

"How did people find out?" I ask.

She clears her throat. "I didn't bleed for three months. I tried to hide my predicament, but Mother found out eventually."

I gape at her. "You're pregnant?"

She shakes her head sadly. "Not anymore."

I grind my teeth. They forced an abortion on her, probably sterilizing her in the process. I feel like breaking something. "What's his name?"

"Excuse me, Sir."

"The jackass who did this to you. What's his name?"

She blinks a few times, surprised I'm insulting the guy instead of her. Then she looks away as though she prefers not to remember.

"William Fox," she replies eventually, her voice cracking on the words.

I do a double-take and study her for a second before a tiny, sad smile rises to my face. "Well, rest assured that William Fox won't harm you ever again, Joy."

She blinks at me again. "What do you mean, Sir?"

"He died when the rebels attacked the camp," I explain with a self-satisfied smile. I wish I could tell her I shot the bastard too, but I can't trust anyone with that information. Fox will have me hung if he ever finds out I'm the one who killed his son.

Joy's eyes widen and I could swear a sparkle of glee shone through her gaze.

"He got what he deserved," she says before catching herself. "I apologize. I shouldn't have said such a horrible thing."

I grin at her. "Your secret is safe with me, Joy."

"You're not like the other officers."

"I sure as hell hope not," I reply before sighing deeply, studying her a bit longer.

"Has anyone touched you since you got here, Joy?"

"Excuse me, Sir?" Her beautiful pale green eyes rise to meet mine.

"Has any guard touched you inappropriately since you got here?"

Her eyes sadden instantly.

"Who was it?" I ask.

"I can't say," she replies. "Please, don't make me tell on him."

I grit my teeth, my nose twitches, and my hands ball into hard fists. "Was it Officer Smith?"

She doesn't reply, but the renewed tears in her eyes speak loud and clear. *I'm gonna kill the douchebag!*

I reach out to wipe off her tears with my thumb, and she looks up at me, her eyes filled with despair.

"He won't be touching you again if he wants to keep his hands, Joy," I tell her. "Now, please go back to work."

She nods while licking her chapped lower lip, before leaving to join the other female prisoners in the field.

171

"Joy," I call out to her.

She turns around and forces herself to look at me.

"Go take a water break," I say. "It's an order, not a request."

She gives me the tiniest smile and heads toward the water fountain in the back of the greenhouse.

I'm suddenly parched too. It's been hot for days and the greenhouse is hardly air-conditioned. I grab a bottle of water and quench my thirst while watching the prisoners. Having to look over them makes me sick, but I can't allow myself to feel for these women. And yet, I still do. No matter how much of my humanity that Fox has managed to rip out, there is still a filament of it left behind that torments me. Enough of it has remained that I can't do this job with serenity. I can't sleep at night peacefully.

I look at the prisoners and imprint their faces in my mind. Their expressions will stay with me forever. When I finally shoot Fox, I will see each one of them roll in front of my eyes.

A shadow moves in my peripheral vision. I react instantly and draw my weapon.

Tina.

I withdraw my rifle.

"Never jump on me like that again when I'm carrying a freaking gun," I berate her.

"I need to talk to you. Tonight. It's important."

"Why not now?"

"I can't. Tonight."

Chapter 30

Stephen - The Next Day

Fox has called me to his office again.

It must be about what Tina said to me last night.

It must be about Chi.

I can't believe he got himself caught a second time. *Does he have a death wish or something?* So much for me trying to protect his ass.

"Stephen." Fox turns to me when I walk in.

He's standing by the window, with his hands held behind his back. I close the door and Fox smiles at me like a carnivorous predator ready to feed.

"We have found your brother at last."

Fox has ensnared his prey. He's satisfied, ready to satiate his hunger.

He licks his lips, almost drooling in thirst for blood.

"He's even more stubborn than you, I'm afraid. Must run in the family." He gives a small laugh and my skin crawls.

He pauses dramatically. He's such a lame actor, even though this role was apparently written just for him.

"I thought Chi might be more willing to answer if you were the one questioning him. He's quite reluctant, but I thought maybe you could get the information I need out of him. It won't be easy. But if you do this, I may give you more freedom than you've had so far. You could have a life outside these walls. For sure, you must be tired of being here. Unable to go as you please, unable to live a normal life."

This is a trap. He'd never let me leave. He doesn't trust me enough for that. *What kind of an idiot does he take me for?*

"I've already tried the chair and the whip. Those didn't work. Maybe you could help me be more creative."

The guy is insane.

Fox is crazier than I thought if he believes I'll follow such idiotic orders. I'm not gonna hurt my brother just because some moron wants me to.

I may hate Chi. But I don't loathe him enough to obey Fox so blindly. When I get back at my brother, it will be on my own terms. It won't be because I'm submitting to some buffoon.

"If you think I'm gonna agree to this, you're a fool," I sneer in his face.

He takes a few steps forward and slaps me so hard I stumble. Then he grabs my cheeks between his fingers and squeezes until I groan.

"I've already had to deal with your brother's insubordination, Stephen. I can guarantee you I am in no mood for your attitude. You may want to reconsider. I'm starting to lose patience."

I pull my face out of his grasp, but I don't respond. The guard by the door is already pointing his gun at my head.

"Now..." Fox resumes his theatrical charade. "I have a second offer for you. You may want to think about it before you reject such an opportunity. I know the rebels will come for your brother eventually. They already saved him once. They will try to do it again. You see, Chi is important to them."

Fox studies my reactions. I give him none.

"When they come to free your brother, I will need you to trade places with him. I will need you to infiltrate the Underground from within and feed me back as much information as possible. There is this rebel I've been looking for. None of my spies have managed to locate him. The Underground leaders are keeping that information a secret because this man is essential to their cause. He has broken through our computerized system a few times, and he needs to be taken down for good. His name is Neil Wilcox."

Fox watches me, as if he's trying to gauge if I recognize the name. When I don't react, he continues, "For two years your brother was hiding right under my nose, at Wilcox's place. Your parents chose the one person who could truly protect your brother and hide his identity. Too bad your brother is so full of himself that he had to come after my son's fiancée." Fox sighs. "Chi refuses to divulge Wilcox's location. That's where you come in to play. The task I have

175

for you is extremely simple. I want you to infiltrate the Underground. You will pretend to be Chi until you find out where that man is hiding."

He pats me on the cheek disdainfully, shooting me a wicked smile.

"What makes you think I'll cooperate?" I ask.

"Stephen, we both know what your brother means to you. I've seen how hard you've tried to protect him. The scars you carry are a clear testimony of that."

I shouldn't care about Chi.

I shouldn't.

I don't.

I don't.

I don't care about him at all.

Liar.

"That was a while ago. Why should I care what happens to him?" I reply. "Maybe I don't want to protect him anymore."

Fox smirks. "Do you really want me to test that theory?"

When I don't reply, his nasty grin widens.

"I've used my techniques on many people, Stephen. Most of them did endure the torture for a while, but you...You were so resistant I thought you'd never let go. It took two months to force you to open up. I don't know if it's the twin thing, but your love for Chi runs deep. And that same love will be your downfall someday."

I clench my teeth.

I don't care about Chi.

Then why are you agreeing to this?

Tina told me she's coming to rescue Chi tomorrow.

This is me betraying her, lying to her, and acting behind her back. But I don't have a choice. I don't fully trust her. Only I can protect Chi, and Tina cannot be involved.

If I am to do this, I can't tell her the truth when it happens. I'm not even sure I can deceive her. I'm not sure I'll be able to fool her long enough to bring back any information.

But this is the only way to protect Chi.

Why do you care?

I don't have time to think about it twice.

I look at Fox. "What about Chi? Where will he go?"

"Your brother will be kept here as a guarantee. Don't screw this up, Stephen, or you will lose more than you've bargained for."

"I need to know that you won't touch him."

He huffs with disgust. "That's really not your call, Stephen. I've been looking for your brother for a very long time. He deserves the punishment."

"If you want the location of that guy, Neil Wilcox, I need to know that Chi will be safe. Lay one finger on him and the deal is off."

Fox raises an eyebrow at me like I'm an idiot.

"You have quite a big mouth, Stephen. But I agree not to touch your brother as long as you get back to me on time with something I can actually use."

Something flickers through his eyes. I don't trust him, but what else am I supposed to do?

"However, if you spend too long without contacting me, your brother will pay the consequences."

I grit my teeth.

"I'll come back to check on him," I say. "You'd better keep your word."

Fox huffs. "You're in no place to make threats, Stephen. Don't test my patience." He sighs. "I'm afraid we have to be a bit rough on you, though. Chi wouldn't cooperate and you have to play the part."

He flashes me a sadistic smile and shrugs as if beating me up is just simple routine. I guess it has come to that point.

Fox presses a digit on his phone.

"It's time," he says.

The door opens a few minutes later and Smith walks in. *You have got to be kidding me!* I didn't sign up for this.

Smith smirks at me and I don't have time to react before he launches himself at me and hits me in the face.

"I've been waiting for this for a very long time," he snickers, holding me by the collar of my shirt.

I ball my fists, but say nothing. *After I take Fox down, Smith is next on my list.*

In my peripheral vision, I see Fox flash all his carnivorous teeth at me. This is the most fun he's had in a while.

Chi owes me a big one for this. He'd better be ready when I come collect my due.

Turncoats

and

Defectors

This scene starts the evening of Thia and William's prenuptial night, after William comes to tell his father that Thia has run away with Chi.

Dimitri Fox stood in front of the camera.

"Is it on?" he asked the man standing behind it.

"Yes, Sir."

The video was being broadcasted in all the police stations in the area. Fox called for his officers' attention as he ordered the search for Chi Richards.

A picture of Chi flashed on the different screens.

"We have reason to believe this boy is highly dangerous. This is the second time he has evaded the law. Proceed with caution. I want him alive. You have one day to find that boy and arrest him, effective immediately."

✳✳✳

The next day, Bryan Harris sighed deeply and braced himself as he faced the door of his boss's office before knocking.

"Come in," a sharp voice called from the inside.

Harris stepped in and lowered his head in deference to Dimitri Fox. The man was sitting at his desk, staring at his computer, and he didn't look up, though he motioned for Harris to come closer.

"What is it, Bryan? I'm busy."

"I apologize, Sir. I thought you might want to know where the boy is hiding."

Fox's eyes rose from the screen. "I'm listening."

"I just received Intel about his current location."

"Hurry up, Harris. I don't have all day," Fox snapped.

"The rebels have a special place for people in need of shelter. Chi is there right now."

"And where is that?" Fox asked.

"In the slums of Eboracum City, Sir. He's staying with a liaison from the Underground. His name is Oliver Wilson. He's a frail, old man. He won't be much trouble when your squad arrives, Sir."

"Is the girl there as well?"

"Yes, Sir."

"I will send a unit right away." Fox grinned at Harris, and the officer couldn't stop the shudder snaking up his spine when he saw the wicked spark in his boss's eye. "It'd better work, Harris. I won't soon forget how you failed me. I've been looking for Chi Richards for two years. You never told me you knew he was part of the Underground."

Bryan Harris didn't respond. As an informant for Fox, his salary was much higher than most officers'. Exposing Chi would have ruined Bryan's position among the rebels. That wasn't a risk he'd been willing to take. But now, his boss knew about Chi, and Bryan's salary would take the hit for his duplicity. He knew that already. He only hoped his boss would leave it at that and not demand further retribution.

"What do you know about Neil Wilcox?" Fox asked.

"Excuse me, Sir?"

"Neil Wilcox, what do you know about him?"

"Isn't he renown for his computer skills, Sir?"

Fox narrowed his eyes. "Are you trying to mess with me, Harris? Or do you really not know Neil's role in the Underground?"

With his mouth gaping open, Bryan stared at his boss.

"You never knew Chi was living with Neil Wilcox and his wife?" Fox asked dubiously. "You never even tried to find out?"

Bryan swallowed hard. "The Underground is protective of its members, Sir. Only the leaders know every rebel under their command. They are the only ones able to contact them all. It is almost impossible to know all their locations. Taylor Jones is secretive about his allies, Sir. He has strict rules concerning privacy. I only know the people closest to him, and that's only because Jones trusts me enough to let me join in on some of their meetings. But I'm not his second in command. If Neil Wilcox is important to the Underground, Jones made sure to hide that fact."

Fox nodded.

"Sir," Harris said, "may I ask why Taylor Jones hasn't been arrested yet?"

Fox let out a tiny grin. "When I take the rebels down, I want to strike hard, Harris. Taking down one leader won't help. Those people are like hydras. You cut a head off and they will just sprout new ones. I don't have time for small talk. Give me the address."

Harris nodded and within minutes, Fox sent his officers out to arrest Chi Richards.

Now, all Harris had to do was send a phone call to Taylor and frame Tina Davis for the whole thing. It hadn't taken long to notice the lack of trust between Taylor and Tina. It wouldn't be hard to convince Taylor that the girl was a turncoat.

Tina was getting too close to the truth. Harris could not afford exposure as a traitor to the rebellion. He would get rid of her first, and then, when the opportunity came, he would take care of Chase Martinez as well. Martinez was a pest and a threat. If Harris's cover got blown, he would lose his position as an officer as well. The stakes were too high.

He would dispose of Tina and Chase, and life would resume its normal course, with luxury and advantages most mortals could only dream of.

***

Over A Week Later

The attacks on the camps had gone as planned.

The various rebel groups would soon fall from the disease. They would be weakened, and Fox would strike when they were at their weakest.

Fox called Harris to his office, and when the officer arrived, he could tell that something was wrong. Fox was sitting behind his desk with feigned placidity, but his restless fingertips were tapping on the armrest of his chair and his eyes were blinking with ticks that showed his profound rage. Harris only hoped his boss's anger had nothing to do with his meeting William Fox a few days before the attack on Camp 19. Harris had heard rumors about the kid's death, and if the rumors were true, Harris's days were counted.

He stood in front of Fox and forced himself to ask, "Sir, when will I be able to advise my family of my well-being? The Underground still believes I'm in custody and my wife is probably frantic."

Fox raised an eyebrow as he glanced at Harris. His cold gaze shot a shiver of fear through the officer, who averted his eyes instantly.

"Tell me, Harris. What happened to Tina Davis?" Fox asked, and the question took Harris by surprise.

He cleared his throat. "Excuse me, Sir?"

"Tina Davis. Would you care to explain to me what happened to her?"

Fox looked at his nails for a few seconds before pinning his cold green eyes on Harris.

Bryan took a deep breath. *How did his boss know about Tina?* Harris had been careful to only involve the Underground. He had made sure they would take Tina down without his boss finding out about it. Fox didn't care much for personal quarrels and retaliations among his officers. Harris knew that, but he did need Tina out of the way.

"I have reason to believe she's working for the rebels, Sir," Harris replied.

Fox tilted his head to the side. "So you decided to take the matter into your own hands without consulting me first?"

Harris lowered his head in submission. "I don't know what you're referring to, Sir."

"Stop taking me for a fool, Harris!" Fox snapped and banged his hand hard on the desk, making Harris jump back in surprise.

"Sir, I had good reason to believe Tina was a Sympathizer working for the rebellion. I only did what was necessary to—
"

"Enough!" Fox shouted. "You don't get to make decisions like these, Harris. I give the orders around here. You jeopardized your own cover without consulting me first. If I had wanted Davis out of the way, the job would be done by now."

"The rebels don't know I'm the one behind her death, Sir."

Fox rose from his seat and stood with both hands propped on his large mahogany desk.

"Her death? You see, Harris, the problem is that Tina is not dead. She is very much alive. She came to me herself to apologize for missing work. The rebels put her in detention and she knows you orchestrated the whole thing. Can you imagine my surprise when she started accusing you of jeopardizing her cover among the rebels?"

"Tina is here?"

Fox looked at Harris sharply and studied his reactions as he turned his computer toward him. A video was playing on the screen, showing Tina meeting with a boy in a cell. When the man's gaze landed on the unfolding scene, his eyes widened. He glanced at Fox before returning his attention to the screen.

"Is this an old video, Sir?" Harris looked at his boss, perplexed.

"Of course not, you idiot," Fox snapped. "Davis came to my office only yesterday, telling me her cover had been blown thanks to you."

Harris's shoulders sagged. This was bad, really bad. But at least this audience wasn't about William. Harris might still be able to make it out of this one. On the video, Tina moved and the boy's face appeared.

"Is that Stephen Richards, Sir? Are they...?"

Fox snickered. "Yes, Bryan. He's banging the girl."

He turned the screen back to its original position and switched the monitor off. Harris cleared his throat with embarrassment.

"Don't be so coy, Bryan. Richards has needs like the rest of us. And Tina Davis is quite an attractive young woman."

Harris averted his eyes. *Where was all this going?*

"So you see, Bryan, Tina came to me, telling me you had tried to blow her cover among the rebels. She said she's still alive only because she's too important for them to kill her so carelessly. And now I am left in quite a predicament because I can't have my officers take each other down behind my back like this. And realistically, I need Tina Davis more than I need you. So what do you advise me to do about this, Harris?"

Fox looked at his employee and waited for an answer, but Harris failed to reply. This meeting was getting worse by the second. Bryan blinked a couple of times, his heart beating fast. When he had taken this job, he hadn't realized that all the luxuries that came with it would quickly become a death trap clutching his throat. But slowly, all the advantages started feeling like quicksand he could no longer escape, like a smothering gift that would kill him if he failed to comply and perform to his boss's expectations. Harris was now thrashing through that same quicksand. He was stuck in it way over his head, ready to suffocate.

Fox was still staring at him. "Tina begged me not to kick her out of her position."

"Sir, I'm positive she's one of them," Bryan tried to explain.

"But you see, Harris, that hardly matters to me. I always choose which information I share with my officers. And I need Tina as leverage against Stephen Richards. The boy is obviously infatuated with her, and she's the only weapon I hold against him right now. And I plan on using every single bullet in my arsenal to subject him to my will, Harris."

"I understand," Harris said with fear in his heart. He could feel his dismissal coming. He was about to lose his job, with all the advantages included.

"Now, that's not why I called you up here, Harris."

Fox's nostrils flared in disgust as he searched his desk drawer for something. He pulled out a gun and raised it, pointing it at Harris's forehead.

Bryan froze.

"What the hell did you tell my son the day he came to speak to you?" Fox asked.

Harris's eyes bulged and his breath caught in his throat.

He didn't answer.

"You have three seconds to answer the damn question, Harris."

191

Bryan didn't move a muscle. His voice wouldn't come out.

Fox started counting. "Three."

Harris tried to breathe. He tried to claw at the voice stuck deep in his throat. He tried to let it out. He wanted to explain.

"Two."

"I..."

"One."

Fox pulled the trigger and Bryan Harris fell.

ACKNOWLEDGMENTS

I would like to thank my husband for being with me on this journey. I know I'm often too busy, too overwhelmed, too distracted by this fictional world, and I thank you for your patience, understanding, and everlasting support. I love you.

A mes parents et à mon frère, merci pour vos encouragements. Merci de m'avoir aidée dans mes études afin que je puisse apprendre l'anglais et écrire ces livres. Je vous aime.

To my mother-in-law, thank you for asking about my books and showing interest. I hope you enjoyed this one as well.

To Jennifer and Josh London, thank you for showing endless support and complimenting my writing even when I think it's dreadful.

To Frankie and Nathan, thank you for supporting the books and spreading the word. Frankie, I am glad you enjoyed the first books. I hope you liked this one, too.

To Nicholas, thank you for following and liking all my pictures and encouraging me. I'm sorry you can't read the books just yet. Just wait a few more years.

To Krista Venero from *Mountains Wanted Publishing*, thank you so much for editing this novella and the short stories. Thanks for the wonderful work and help!

To my author friends, Kathryn Berla, Vera Burris, Claire Kann, Kylie Kaemke, Elizabetta Holcomb, and J. Kahele, thank you for your endless support, for still reading the books, for giving me your input, and for telling me I shouldn't give up.

To Nadège Chrétien, Michèle Chrétien, et Elizabeth Lee, merci pour tous vos encouragements.

To Mikel Tadeje, April Soller, and Sunni Hancock, thank you for going the extra mile to promote my series. I am forever grateful.

A Flo, merci d'avoir lu le livre en anglais. :-)

To all the bloggers who have asked for my books, thank you so much for reading and reviewing. Thank you for your time, and thank you for giving me a chance.

To Evelyn Espada, you are such an inspiration. I apologize for not talking more often, but you never cease to inspire me. :-)

A mes cousines Harbulot, merci pour votre soutien. Je suis désolée d'avoir écrit les livres en anglais. J'espère avoir un jour le temps de les traduire...

To all my readers and those who have picked up this book, thank you so much. My characters are only "alive" because you read their stories.

Finally, to all of Stephen's fans, including Chloe Berger, Tuba Sayed, and Emily Katherine Jinxx, I feel like you have been on Stevie's side since forever. Thank you for loving him unconditionally in spite of his many flaws. I hope he didn't disappoint you in this book and that he answered your many questions.

I am so thankful to anyone who has helped me with this series. Thank you for reading.

I pledge to donate 100% of sales revenue from "Holding Ground" and "Losing Ground" to an anti-sexual violence association. You can find more information about that on my website. If you've received this book for free, please help Stevie donate with a simple download of the ebook.

If, like Stephen, you have gone through pain and abuse, always remember you are not alone. It was *never* your fault. You are a survivor. And you are *always* in my thoughts.

Reach for help:

RAINN:
www.rainn.org
800-656-4673

Child Helpline International:
www.childhelplineinternational.org
+31-20-528-9625

ADDITIONAL MATERIAL

PLAYLIST

Theme Songs:
"Easier To Run" by Linkin Park

"Naked" by Assemblage 23

Stephen:
"Nemo" by Nightwish

"Crawling" by Linkin Park

"See Me in Shadows" by Delain

"Rule The World" by Kamelot

"How Does It Feel" by Avril Lavigne

"Eventually" by P!nk

"Scream" by Halestorm

Stephen and the Richards:
"Virtue to Vice" by Deathstars

"Oh Father" by Madonna

"Haunted" by Evanescence

"Figure.09" by Linkin Park

"You'll See" by Madonna

"Perfect" by Alanis Morissette

"The Power of Goodbye" by Madonna

Stephen and Chi:

"Existence in Progress" by Icon of Coil

"Invisible and Silent" by Covenant

"Mon Frère" by Les Dix Commandements

"From The Inside" by Linkin Park

"Breaking The Habit" by Linkin Park

"Take Me Away" by Avril Lavigne

"Foolish Games" by Jewel

Willow:

"The Voice Within" by Christina Aguilera

"I Will Remember You" by Sarah McLachlan

"Overprotected" by Britney Spears

Stephen and Willow:

"Run to You" by Whitney Houston

"Pas le temps de vivre" by Mylène Farmer

"Innocence" by Avril Lavigne

"Halo" by Beyoncé

"Everytime" by Britney Spears

"Somewhere" by Within Temptation

"My Immortal" by Evanescence

"Memories" by Within Temptation

"Without You" by Mariah Carey

Stephen for Tina:

"Don't Cry" By Guns N' Roses

"Push It" by Garbage

"Hot" by Avril Lavigne

"Lust or Love" by Scorpions

"Cryin'" by Aerosmith

"I Don't Want A Lover" by Texas

"The Bitter End" by Placebo

"It Must Have Been Love" by Roxette

Tina for Stephen:

"All Through the Night" by Cyndi Lauper

"In Your Room" by Halestorm

"Frozen" by Madonna

"Try" by P!nk

"Bad Romance" by Lady Gaga

"Underneath It All" by No Doubt

Dimitri Fox:

"Cyanide" by Deathstars

"Hells Bells" by AC/DC

"The Game" by Motorhead

Holding Ground

Chi

A Short Story 2

Alice Rachel

Chi: A Short Story 2

PART 1: Chi's Childhood

Chi - Seven Years Old

I'm standing by Stephen's bed, staring at him.

"Stephen, are you okay?"

He opens his eyes and nods. Even though he gives me a tiny smile, his skin is pale and he still looks sick.

"I'm feeling better," he says.

Mommy says the fever is gone, but she wants him to stay in bed a few more days. She told me Stephen got something called the West Nile virus. When he was really sick, Stephen barfed a lot and pooped his pants. I wasn't allowed in his room, and I cried and cried every night because I didn't want him to die.

"I miss you," I say, because it's true I miss him and I miss playing with him, even though he always wins when we play, and I hate it when he beats me at board games. I know he cheats, but I still like playing with him.

I sit on the bed and give him a big hug. He pats me on the back and returns my hug.

"I love you, and you're not allowed to die," I say. "We made a pact, remember?"

"I'm not dead," he replies.

"No, but you almost died, and you're not allowed! Because we promised. You and me together forever. Remember?"

He snorts. "Dork."

"Wanna play checkers?" I ask.

He shrugs. "Okay. Are you gonna cry if I win? 'Cause I'm gonna win and you know it." He gives me a smile.

I puff up my chest. "I don't cry. I'm a big boy. And big boys don't cry. Daddy told me that real men never cry."

"You do too cry," Stephen replies. "And I saw Daddy cry once, too."

"No, I don't. And no, he didn't. He's a man and men don't cry."

Stephen shrugs. "You cry all the time."

"C'est pas vrai!" *That's not true!*

The door opens and Daddy walks in.

"Chi, it's time for bed. I need a moment with Stephen."

"But we were gonna play checkers," I protest.

Daddy gives me the big eyes—the big scary look he uses when I don't obey. He hates it when I whine, but I wanna spend more time with Stephen.

"Chi, I won't ask you twice."

My shoulders sag. "Fine."

"See you tomorrow, Baby Brother," Stephen says, with a huge hug so tight I can't breathe.

Ugh, I hate it when he calls me that. "I'm the same age as you!" I puff my chest again.

"You were born second. So you're my baby brother."

I pout, but Daddy glares at me. "Chi, time for bed."

"Okay, okay."

I stand up and walk past Daddy, who comes to sit next to Stephen. He holds out a present to him, and Stephen opens his eyes wide with glee.

"Is this for me, Daddy?" he asks.

"Of course, a present for my special boy," Daddy replies and ruffles Stephen's hair.

Stephen smiles wider. "Is it a book, Daddy?"

"Maybe? What do you think?" Daddy winks at him.

My heart squeezes a bit. Daddy never gives me any presents. Except on my birthday. And he never calls me his special boy either. I stand by the door and watch as Stephen opens his present.

It is a book!

Stephen loves books. He collects them, and sometimes he gets in big trouble because he takes Mommy's books from her shelves, and then he gets grounded for a week. Daddy takes Stephen to the bookstore every week, but he never takes me. He says it's too dangerous because I'm an Unwanted and I'm not supposed to be alive. I told Daddy I could pretend to be Stephen and I'd walk like Stephen and talk like Stephen and everything too, but Daddy said I'd never be Stephen and that pretending was just no good.

Stephen looks up at Daddy and leans forward to give him a hug.

"Thank you, Daddy," he says. "Thank you, thank you!"

207

Daddy turns around to look at me. "What are you still doing here, Chi? I thought I told you to go to bed."

He rises to his feet and walks toward me to push me out of the room. He closes the door in my face without looking at me. There's something in my chest, like a ball, and I can feel a sob coming. But I will not cry. Big boys don't cry. I blink hard. I know Daddy doesn't love me as much as he loves Stephen.

I breathe in deep and lean against the doorframe, pressing my ear hard against the wood to listen.

Daddy's voice comes through the door. "Daddy loves you, Stephen. You know that, right?"

"Yes, Daddy." Stephen giggles as if Daddy is tickling him.

"I found a special place in the woods where there's a little stream with tiny fish and frogs. We can go there when you're fully recovered. Just you and me. It'll be our secret place, and we won't tell Chi or Mommy about it."

"But I want Chi to come fish with us," Stephen says.

"You don't want to spend time alone with your old man?" Daddy asks.

"Yes, Daddy, I do. I love fishing with you the best. Chi always cries if I catch lots of fish."

"So, you won't tell Chi or Mommy?" Daddy asks. "I can trust you, right? It will be our little secret."

Stephen giggles. "Okay, Daddy."

"I need to go for now, but I will come back a bit later tonight. There's something special I want to share with you. We can celebrate your recovery. We'll have a little party of our own. But it has to be our secret. You promise you won't tell Chi and Mommy?"

"Yes, Daddy, it will be our secret."

Feeling sad, I sigh and take a step back from the door. I guess it's fine if they have secrets. After all, I have Mommy all to myself most of the time and she loves me very much. When Stephen is at school and Daddy is at work, Mommy spends all day with me. Only me. So, I guess it's okay if Stephen is Daddy's special boy.

✳✳✳

A Couple Of Weeks Later

When I get downstairs, I walk in on Stephen eating cereal at the kitchen table. I run to him and give him a big hug.

"You're all better! You're all better! You're finally out of your room!"

He gives me a look and shrugs.

"Why are you sad? Aren't you better?"

He shrugs again and gives me a tiny smile, but it doesn't look like a real happy smile.

"Are you going back to school?" I ask.

"Mommy said I could go back next week."

I squeal and jump up and down a few times. "So you're gonna be here, and we can spend all day playing? Can we play wrestle?"

Stephen stares at me like I'm crazy. "Mommy said I'm gonna study with you."

"Awww." I slouch my shoulders.

"I thought you loved studying?" he asks.

"I do, but I wanted to play with you."

Stephen takes a bite out of his cereal and makes lots of crunchy noises. I see the book on the side of the table.

"Can I borrow it sometime?" I ask.

Stephen looks at the book and makes a face. "You can have it. It's stupid anyway."

I stare at him, but he looks away sadly.

"Are you okay?" I ask.

"Yes, I'm fine," he says, but he bites his lower lip like he wants to cry and he blinks fast, fast, fast.

Then he pushes his bowl away and stands up. He leaves without looking at me. He didn't eat much of his food. If Mommy sees this, she won't be happy. We are not allowed to waste resources. And especially not special items like milk. I sit in his chair and eat his cereal. This way, Mommy won't know that Stephen didn't finish his breakfast. I grab the book that Daddy gave Stephen: *Danny the Champion of the World*. I don't know why Stephen doesn't like the book; it looks fun to me.

***

Chi - Ten Years Old

I'm almost asleep when someone knocks on my bedroom door and tries to turn the knob. I sit up. *The officers are here to snatch me! They've found me. They've come for me.*

My heart jumps and jumps. My chest hurts. I don't dare turn on the light, even though Mom told me to hide in my closet if the officers ever came for me. My heart races, races, races.

But then I hear Stephen's voice. "Chi, are you awake?"

I breathe with relief. It's only Stephen.

He tries my door again, but I've locked it like Mom told me to. She said the officers can't come and snatch me if the door is locked. Stephen knocks on my door again, and I stand up and walk over to open it. As soon as he sees me, Stephen scurries inside and closes the door behind us.

"Can I sleep here tonight?" he asks.

"Why? What's wrong with your room?"

He doesn't reply, but a slight shiver shakes his body.

"Are you scared of them, too?" I ask.

"Who?"

"The officers," I explain.

Stephen stares at me and then at the lock.

"Does it work?" he asks.

"What?"

"The lock, does it work?" he asks again.

I nod and he turns the bolt. Then he tries to pull the door open a few times. When he sees that no one can come in, he looks at me again.

"So, can I sleep here tonight?"

"Mom said you're supposed to say 'may,' not 'can' when you want permission for something."

He huffs at me and rolls his eyes. "I take that as a yes," he says and walks toward my bed.

My bed is tiny. I don't really want to share it with Stephen, but he looks tired. I know he doesn't sleep well. Maybe if he spends the night here, he'll feel better. I asked Mom why Stephen doesn't have a lock on his door, and she said the officers don't want Stephen, they want me. I tried to protest, but she wasn't too happy when I insisted that he should have a lock, too.

She said, "I already have to stay home all day to take care of you. We can never go anywhere. I'm not getting a bolt for Stephen when he's free to go as he pleases. He's luckier than us."

I dropped the matter after that. I didn't tell Mom that her words pained me and made my chest hurt.

But if the officers don't want Stephen, then why is he so scared all the time?

I look at him with sad eyes as he sits on my bed. It's my fault Stephen is scared. It's my fault the officers found out about us and we had to move here, away from home.

"Okay, you can sleep here," I reply. "But don't hog the sheets."

He leaves his old slippers by the bed and holds his stuffed bunny, Floppy Puff Puff, close to his chest. I've never seen Stephen go to bed without Floppy. His bunny is grayish, old, and falling apart, but Stephen loves that thing. I can't blame him; I sleep with my blanky every night, too. Mom said we're too old for that stuff, but the blanket makes me feel safe, and Stephen threw a fit when Mom wanted to get rid of his bunny.

Stephen is wearing his blue striped pajamas, and he asks which side he can take. Considering he's already sitting on the left side, I don't know why he's asking.

"It doesn't matter. Just leave me some space."

I slip under the covers and pull them up all the way to my chin. Stephen settles next to me. We can hardly fit in the bed together, so we have to sleep on our sides, back to back.

"Chi?" he whispers in the dark.

"Yeah."

"Does Dad come into your room to check on you at night?"

"No. Why?"

Stephen shrugs against my back. "Nothing. Just wondering."

A pang of grief pulls at my chest. I know Dad cares more about Stephen. And now I know he even checks on him at night, probably to make sure he's safe. I pull my blanky tight against me and try not to suck my thumb like I used to when I was really little. Mommy said it's a nasty habit that'll mess up my teeth. But when I'm really sad or really stressed out, I still do it when no one's watching.

After that, Stephen doesn't say anything more and before long, we both fall asleep.

In the middle of the night, I fall to the ground and wake in a somersault. Stephen has moved too much and pushed me off the bed.

"What the heck?!"

I turn on the light and look at him, but he's still sleeping. *No fair!* I lean over him and grab his shoulder to shake him awake. But when I touch him, Stephen opens his eyes wide with fear and starts thrashing at me violently.

"Don't touch me!" he screams and slaps me in the face.

I stand there, stunned, and hold my cheek. *Don't cry! Be a big boy! Don't cry!* My lips are shaking. And I blink, but the tears still come out.

"I never want you to sleep in my room again," I yell at him.

Stephen looks at me and rubs his eyes, like he doesn't know what's going on. "What happened?"

"As if you don't know." *He did it on purpose!* "Go back to your room! This is my room and I don't want you here!"

He stares at me with sudden terror. "Don't yell like that, Chi. You'll wake him up and then he'll know I'm here."

"Get out of my room!" I shout.

"Please, stop yelling," he begs, his eyes filling with tears. "Please, don't make me go back there. I'll be good. I can

214

sleep on the floor if you want. I get terrible nightmares," he explains quickly. "Can I stay? Please."

I really don't want him in my room anymore, but I'm surprised at how he's panicking. He looks so scared, I can't say no. He probably thinks the officers are gonna come and snatch him in the middle of the night.

I sigh. "Okay, for tonight. But tomorrow, you're sleeping in your room. And if you push me off the bed again, you're out."

I don't have the heart to make him sleep on the floor, so I lie down next to him again. Instead of turning his back to me, Stephen snuggles against me and wraps his arm around my stomach. His nightmare must have been real scary 'cause Stephen doesn't like to cuddle. I don't say anything, though. I'm too tired to fight him anyway. I nestle against him and fall asleep quickly.

***

The Next Day

"**Chi, get ready,**" Dad says when I head down the stairs with Stephen at the end of the day. Dad is back from work, and yesterday, he promised we'd go hunting for our dinner. We're all going, which is a real event because Stephen and I aren't usually allowed outside at the same time.

I give a fist pump and high five Stephen.

215

Once we get to the foyer, Stephen reaches down for his shoes.

"You're not coming, Stephen," Dad says harshly.

Stephen looks at Dad and blinks. "Why not?"

"Because you were a mean little boy last night. I don't feel like being around you right now."

Stephen's eyes well up. "What did I do, Daddy?"

"I think you know what you did," Dad replies, narrowing his eyes so much that Stephen takes a step back. "Maybe you should go to your room and ponder your actions for a while, huh? Think about how mean you were to your poor Daddy who does so much for you every day."

I don't remember what Stephen did yesterday, but he must have done something really, really bad 'cause he's Dad's favorite. Dad always gives him presents and lots of stuff he never gives me, and he hardly ever punishes Stephen.

"Daddy, please, I want to come with you and Chi," Stephen pleads.

"No," Dad responds.

Mom enters the room and gives Stephen an angry look. Stephen is in deep trouble. That's probably why he wanted to sleep in my room last night. He lied to me. He wasn't scared of the officers; he was scared because he knew he had done something really bad and Daddy was going to punish him.

"Go to your room, Stephen," Mom says.

216

"You're going, too?" he asks when Mom puts on one of her shoes.

"Yes," she replies.

Mom never goes if Dad takes Stephen out, though. Another proof that Daddy loves Stephen more. I know he wants to spend time alone with him and not with me. I know they go to that secret place by the stream—the one I heard them talk about. Daddy never takes me there. The one time I asked about it, he got really angry and told me to mind my own business.

I give Stephen a sad look, but he glares at me.

Dad leans close to Stephen's ear. "You and I will have a talk tonight, young man."

Stephen whimpers and blinks like he wants to cry, and then he runs through the hall and up the stairs, screaming the whole time that he hates all of us and he hopes we die. My heart aches. I hate it when my brother wishes our parents dead.

The sound is loud when he slams his bedroom door. Mom rolls her eyes, pulls me close to her, and bends down before kissing my forehead.

"Sois gentil avec papa et maman, mon ange." *Be nice to Mommy and Daddy, my angel.* "Your brother doesn't understand we already have enough to deal with. With you being illegal, life is difficult enough as it is. We deserve better than those nasty tantrums he throws all the time."

Mom's words sting me a bit, but I nod. I want Mom and Dad to be happy. I know it's my fault things are so hard for them. I wish Stephen tried to be nicer sometimes. I smile at Mom and she pats me on the head.

"Come on now, mon chou, let's go hunt."

***

When we get back home, Stephen is waiting at the top of the stairs. I can tell from his red, blotchy face that he has cried a lot. He gives me a sad look and my heart hurts for him. I show him a tiny smile that he returns with a scowl of his own.

"Go to your room, Stephen," Dad says.

"May I come back down for dinner?" Stephen asks.

"No."

"But Daddy, I'm hungry," Stephen replies.

"You were a mean little boy. Go to your room. I won't say it twice," Dad snaps at him.

"I'm sorry I said I hated you. Please, I'm hungry, Daddy." He looks at the rabbit hanging from Dad's fist and his eyes sadden even more.

"Go to your room, Stephen," Dad repeats.

Meat is Stephen's favorite meal—any kind of meat. Mom said meat is a luxury, and Stephen always eats it slowly while making sounds the entire time like he loves it so much.

Stephen turns around and leaves, his shoulders dropping with grief. Daddy shakes his head and huffs.

After that, dinner is quiet and I'm not hungry at all. I hate it when Stephen is naughty and gets punished. I hate it when he's sad. There is always this pain in my chest when that happens, and I don't understand it.

✱✱✱

When it's dark, I grab my flashlight and go to lean against my bedroom door. I listen to hear if Mom and Dad are in their room. I take a breath as I unlatch the lock. *What if the officers are here and want to take me away?* My heart races fast, fast, fast, and there's another pain in my chest I can't explain, but I know Stephen is hurting and I want him to feel better.

I open the door and puff my chest. I'm a big boy. I can do this. I cast a glance down the hall just as Stephen's door opens and Dad walks out. I hide real quick in my own room and close the door. I almost got caught. I'll be in big trouble if Dad catches me sneaking food into Stephen's room. I breathe hard, with my back against the door. And I wait. I wait for a long time.

When I'm sure Dad won't leave his room again, I tiptoe my way down the hall and then down the stairs. I hear a noise and freeze. I move the flashlight around, but I see nothing, so I go to the kitchen and open the fridge. Mom put the leftovers right there, on the middle shelf.

I grab a chair so I can reach the cupboard way up. I climb on the chair, but when I grab a plate, I almost drop it. The fridge is still open. Its light is coming out and helps me see better. I make my way down the chair and go to pick up a rabbit leg from the plate in the fridge. There are lots of apples in there, too. Mommy must have picked them up from the trees in our backyard. I grab one. I hope Mommy doesn't notice that it's gone, or I'll be in big trouble.

When my plate is covered with food, I tiptoe my way back upstairs and turn the knob on Stephen's door. I step inside and hear a whimper and then a sob.

"Stephen, it's me," I whisper.

I hear a noise like he's blowing his nose.

"May I turn on the light?" I ask.

He doesn't reply. He's still crying and I think he's trying hard not to because it sounds like he's choking.

I turn on the light and he's lying on his stomach, definitely crying in his pillow. My heart squeezes and squeezes. I hate it when my brother hurts.

"Stephen?"

I walk to the bed and sit by his side. He quickly wipes off his tears and turns around to look at me. I hand him the plate, but he shakes his head.

"I don't want anything the witch cooked," he says. The witch is what Stephen calls Mom when he's really mad at her. But I can tell from the way he's staring at the plate that he's hungry.

I put the plate on my lap. Stephen can be stubborn, but if I eat in front of him, he won't resist for long. I grab the rabbit leg and bite into it.

"Mmm, so yummy," I say, my eyes never leaving his sad face. I make lots of sounds with my mouth like it's real

220

good, and Stephen looks at me with big round eyes like he's starving.

Then he caves in and takes the plate from my hands. He starts eating, slowly at first, and then real quick like he's super hungry and worried I might take the plate away. Every so often, his chest rises with a hiccup because he was crying so hard earlier. He eats quickly, without taking his time like he usually does.

I smile at him the entire time, and when he's done, he gives me a tiny smile, too.

"Thank you."

"You're welcome." I raise my fist and Stephen bumps his against mine. "Wanna play a game?" I ask.

He shrugs. "I'm tired."

"You're okay?" I ask.

He looks at me with big, dark, sad eyes. "Yeah. Don't tell Mom I ate tonight."

I nod.

✱✱✱

"You stole the food," Mom yells from the kitchen. "Nasty little thief."

"No, I didn't," Stephen replies.

"Then, how come I'm missing an apple and a rabbit leg? Little liar."

I walk in. "I ate those, Mommy," I say. "I was still hungry and I ate the leg and the apple. I'm sorry. I know I'm not allowed to eat more than my share." I lower my eyes, ashamed because I'm lying. I love my Mommy. I hate lying to her. But the truth is I love my brother more.

"You don't need to cover up for him, mon ange," she says.

"I'm not. I ate the food."

"Is it true, Stephen?" she asks, sending him a sharp glance.

Stephen gives me a look and I nod at him, but he must not have understood my message because he shakes his head and says, "No, I ate it."

Mommy nods like she already knew I was lying, but I repeat, "Non, c'était moi." *No, I did it.*

She sighs and I can tell she's getting angry. "Est-ce que je dois vous punir tous les deux, alors?" *Should I punish the two of you, then?*

I shake a little because I hate it when Mommy punishes me. It doesn't happen often, but she's never nice when she catches me being naughty.

Stephen stands up for me. "No, Chi didn't do anything."

"There will be no dessert for you two, and that's a shame because I was going to make Chi's favorite."

I swallow hard as I remember the apples in the fridge. Mom is going to make an apple pie and I won't get any of it. I try hard not to cry, and Stephen clenches his jaw.

"You're mean. You're mean, mean, mean, and I hate you!" he yells at Mom. "I don't want your stupid pie. I don't want anything made by you. You're probably poisoning my food with your mean meanness. I hate you!"

He storms out of the room, and Mom lets out a sob.

"I'm sorry I disobeyed, Mommy," I say.

She glances at me. "Go to your room and think about what you did. I have sacrificed so much for you, Chi. I believe I deserve better."

I turn around and leave the kitchen with tears in my eyes and something painful pulling at my chest.

PART 2: Chi's Teenage Years

Chi - Seventeen Years Old

The chickens in Willow's barn peep when I stand up and embrace her while wrapping the sheet around us. She blushes and looks away sadly.

"Are you okay, Will?"

She nods and gives me a smile that never reaches her eyes.

"You've been awfully sullen recently."

I lift her chin and meet her blue, sorrow-filled gaze, and I have a strange feeling that I'm the one who put all the grief there.

"No, I'm okay," she says.

She's lying. I know that. But I don't know what's wrong or why she's lying about it.

"Why are you so sad? Did I do something wrong?"

She shakes her head and bites her lower lip. She forces a smile when I stroke her cheek and kiss her jaw.

"Our marriage, it won't ever be real, right?" she asks.

"What do you mean?"

"Well, you and I, we're illegal. We're not supposed to exist, so our marriage won't be recognized by the state. Technically, it won't be valid."

"Is that what saddens you?" I ask and tighten our embrace.

She doesn't reply.

"I'm illegal. Does it mean I'm not real to you?" I ask.

She looks at me and pats my face as if to check that I am, indeed, real.

"Yes, you are real," she confirms.

"Our marriage will be real if we want it to be."

She shrugs and looks away again. I can't stand to see her so sad. *Why won't she tell me what's wrong?*

"Have you changed your mind? We don't need to go through with it if you don't want to."

"Will Stephen and Lila have a real wedding?" she asks.

Is that why she's been so sullen? She thinks Lila will have a beautiful ceremony that she won't get to be a part of.

"Their paperwork will be official, but my mom said they'll get married the same day we do. So, they won't have an official ceremony."

Willow gasps and her eyes well up.

"No one told me that," she says. "Did your mom discuss this with my parents? I mean, that we'll get married on the same day?"

"Not yet. But I doubt there'll be a wedding, Will. I mean, for Stephen. He refuses to date Lila. My parents would have to drag him there screaming. He's..." I pause. "He's not really what I'd call easy to handle."

Her chest rises and falls against mine. I can tell she's trying not to cry, so I pull her face against my shoulder and stroke the back of her head.

"I will take good care of you, Willow, I promise. I will always respect you and treat you well."

She nods against my shoulder.

"Will you tell me why you're so sad?" I ask again. "Is it really because we won't get an official ceremony? 'Cause if it's that, we can make it as beautiful as you want it to be, I swear."

She nods, but something still resides deep inside her eyes. Whatever it is that's grieving her, she won't open up about it.

She is to be my wife, whether the state recognizes our marriage as valid or not, and I want her to be happy. She's the sweetest girl I know. Well, I guess she's the only girl I know—besides Lila of course. But Willow is the gentlest person I've ever met. If anyone deserves happiness, it's definitely her. I hate that she's forced to hide. I hate that she never got a chance at a normal life.

"Where will we live?" she asks. "We won't be able to own a house. Maybe you should date a girl who could hide you and protect you. Someone legal."

"I don't want you to worry about all that. We'll make it work. My parents know people. They can give us false identities. We can live in society like normal people and pretend we were born legally. I want you to have a normal life, Will. You *deserve* a normal life."

"You could marry a legal girl under a false identity too," she says.

"I don't wanna have to lie to my potential wife."

226

"What if she already knew about your status?"

I look at her and blink. *Where is all this coming from?*

"Willow, I'm not marrying anyone but you. If you will have me, of course."

She nods, but I'm not sure she's still on board with this plan. I won't marry her if she doesn't want me, though. I've already told her that many times. I don't know how to make myself any clearer, but I'm too selfish to break up with her if she won't break it off first. She's the only companion I have. She's my only friend. Losing her would be more painful than she thinks.

I kiss her temple and whisper in her ear, "Will you spend your life with me, Will? Be mine and I will be yours, always. I promise."

She breathes deeply and is about to reply when a sound interrupts her. Someone's at the door.

"Get dressed!" I whisper in a rush. "I don't want your mom to catch us like this."

She half-sobs, half-chuckles. "Chi, we are to be married. I'm sure she knows this is bound to happen at some point."

"Still, I'd rather she didn't catch us naked together."

Willow blinks and flushes as I cup her face before kissing her. I am so lucky to be engaged to a girl like her. I will make sure her life is the best I can provide.

***

The Next Day

"**What did you do** with the animal encyclopedia, Stephen?" Mom shrieks with anger.

Stephen doesn't reply. He sneers at her and crosses his arms over his chest. "What makes you think I took it? I have no use for your stupid books."

He's lying. He loves to read, and he was heartbroken when we moved eight years ago and Mom decided to leave half our library behind.

"I can just go through your room when you're at school. You know that, right?"

Stephen's eyes darken. "Sure, whatever. You and Father both just come to my room whenever you damn well please. The door is wide open. You're sick. The two of you. You know that?"

Mom clenches her jaw. "Apologize this instant."

"Go to hell!"

Mom narrows her eyes like she could kill him. "By the way," she says, "I found the drawing you were hiding in your nightstand table."

Stephen's face turns deathly pale, and he doesn't reply. He runs out of the living room without looking back. His feet pound against the stairs before he reaches the second floor and enters his room. We can hear him shuffling through his stuff and throwing it all around. Then his footsteps echo back down the stairs, and loud French curses come pouring out of his mouth like a torrent of hatred. He enters the living room again and takes one warning step toward Mom. I'm afraid I'll have to interfere. Stephen has never touched Mom. Not once. I don't think he ever would, but when they start, their fights get nasty.

"Stephen..." I say.

He cuts me a quick, sharp glance. "Stay out of it, Chi." His gaze turns to Mom. "What did you do with it?"

Mom raises an eyebrow. "Give me back the encyclopedia, Stephen. I need it for your brother's tutoring."

"Give me back the picture right now," Stephen snarls.

He takes an ominous step forward and stands in Mom's face. He's far enough that he's not touching her, but I still walk between them and push him away. I'm sick of living in this broken home.

"Get the hell out of my face, Chi," he snaps at me.

I press my hand to his chest, trying to keep him away from Mom.

"Do you have the encyclopedia?" I ask him, softly.

"Sure, just side with her," he growls. "Like you always do."

I grit my teeth. I wouldn't side with Mom if he didn't act like such a jerk all the time.

"Give me back that damn picture!" he screams at Mom.

"Calm down, Stephen," I hiss at him, now growing seriously pissed. She's my mother too, and I won't let anyone talk to her like that.

"It's all I have left," Stephen tells Mom in a broken voice, his eyes suddenly pleading. "And you know it."

I take a second glance at him, taken aback by his sudden mood swing. Stephen is like a wind vane, turning and spinning, unpredictable. His tantrums are often followed by instant pain and sorrow. But no matter how much I try to reason with him, nothing ever seems to stop him from lashing out at Mom.

His eyes well up slightly, but he blinks fast and his gaze turns dark and cold.

"Haven't you taken enough from me already?" he snaps.

And then, he breaks down, falls to his knees, and starts crying—real tears. *What the hell is going on?* Stephen never cries like this.

"Give me back the picture, Mom, please. Please, it's all I have."

I look at Mom, but she has turned her back to Stephen. "Mom?" I ask. "What picture is he talking about?"

She looks at me sadly. "He can't have it back until he brings back what he has stolen. We need that encyclopedia. Encyclopedias are illegal; I can't get another one. Stephen knows how precious it is. Stealing is wrong."

I turn to Stephen, who rises to his feet. His eyes are still pouring tears, but there's something dangerous in them too, like lightning and ravaging fire.

230

"You'll never see that damn encyclopedia again. You've stolen more from me than I've stolen from you. I hate you! All of you!"

With that, he storms out of the room and slams the door so hard that the window pane shatters. Mom gasps and clutches her chest. She's breathing funny.

"Mom, are you okay?"

She shakes her head. "I can't. I can't control him anymore. Oh, Chi..." She falls into my arms and cries against my shoulder. "What did I ever do to him?"

"It's okay, Mom. I'll talk to him. I'm sure he'll give it back if I ask nicely." I'm lying. He'll tell me to go to hell, like he always does. "And even if he doesn't, I know a lot about nature already. Willow is teaching me many things. We don't need that book."

She shakes her head against my neck and I pat her back. "I love you, Mom. You know that, right?"

She nods and cups my cheeks, her eyes roaming my face. "My sweet, sweet boy. What would I ever do without you?"

"It'll be fine, Mom, I promise."

My heart is in shreds. My brother is tearing my family apart. *What did we do to him to deserve this?* I'm just sick of it. I'm sick of him. And his attitude.

I clench my teeth and look at the door Stephen just destroyed. I let go of Mom and head out of the room with my hands balled into tight fists as I walk down the hall, up the stairs, all the way to Stephen's bedroom.

I don't knock. I don't give a damn if he's mad. I step into his room without asking if that's okay. He will apologize to Mom whether he wants to or not.

When I walk in, Stephen is standing by the window. I throw him a nasty glare, but I'm forced to change my stance when I find him looking outside, with his shoulders shaking hard. He's still crying furiously and the sight stings my soul.

The drawer of his nightstand table has been thrown face down on his bed, and everything it contained is scattered all over the floor—papers, notes, a couple of books. His room is a mess. It's like a tornado came right through here. Stephen is always such a neat freak. The sight of such destruction is unsettling.

Though I had come here to confront him, the violent shakes of his body and the sounds of his sobs draw me to him, so I have to comfort him instead.

Stephen has been in pain for a very long time. I can feel his emotions as if they were my own. His pain flows through my skin as if we shared the same body. And I hurt just from looking at him. But he won't talk to me. He's making our lives so difficult. I've asked him if there was anything bad going on at school, or if there was anything I could do to help, but all he ever does is push me away.

He can be such an asshole.

But he is my brother.

And I won't let go.

No matter how hard he pushes me away, I am right here and I'm not leaving. Even when he's a storm lashing at me with raging thunder, I still hold on and I won't let go.

"Stephen?"

He doesn't acknowledge me, except for one word that he spits out with rage: "Dégage!" *Get the hell out.*

I walk over and force him to turn around and look at me. He tries to push me back, but I stand my ground as he looks at me like he wants to kill me. And there are times when I almost think that he might actually do it, that he might actually kill me. But he has never touched me. Not first, at least. The only time he did punch me was because I'd triggered the fight and hit him.

"Where do you think she hid it?" he asks, out of the blue.

"What?"

"The drawing, where would she put it? Do you think she destroyed it?" he adds, his eyes red-rimmed. "Maybe it's in her room."

My heart aches, constantly torn between him and Mom. *Why can't they get along? Just once. Please. Is that really too much to ask?*

"I don't even know what drawing you're talking about, Stephen."

His shoulders slump forward from a heavy sigh.

"It's all I have left," he says and turns toward the window again. "She took everything from me. I need that drawing."

I shake my head. *What is he talking about?* I can't help him find the drawing if he won't tell me what it is.

"Why do you say you have nothing? You have me," I reply. "I don't know what you're talking about, Stephen. You've always had me and you still do. I'm here. I'm right here for you. What's this drawing you're talking about?"

He throws me a look over his shoulder, the sadness in his eyes real and deep. "Please leave," he says in a broken voice.

I would push him further, but the pain in his voice is so sharp and cutting that I'm forced to relent. I don't want to upset him any more than he already is. I give him one last glance, but he's no longer looking at me.

One single sob shakes him as he tightens his hands on both sides of his body while pressing his forehead against the window. He stays like that and doesn't seem to notice that I haven't even left yet. I can't stand to watch him behave like this, not when he won't let me help. I leave because he asked me to, but my heart is crushed.

When Mom is busy, I'll go through her stuff and see if I can find that picture. Or maybe I can sway her into giving it back.

✳✳✳

Three Months Later - At The Wilcoxes' House

Jane turns on the news, and Willow's face pops up on the screen. I stop what I'm doing and stare at the TV. The journalist talks as shots of Willow's house flash on the screen in front of my eyes, and then there's a view of her kitchen floor, covered with blood. My heart races. *Willow! No!* The man on the news goes on and on about the vicious killings that took Willow's life and her parents' too.

The man on TV says my name next, and I blink a few times as he points at a blurry picture that he claims to be me. It does looks like a picture of me, I guess, but it's too blurry to tell. Another picture of me appears—this one clearer. The boy in the shot has been pinned against the wall by someone forcing his head back, but his face is all twisted with anger. It would be hard for anyone who doesn't know that person to recognize him.

It's a picture of Stephen. There is no doubt about it. That is my brother right there on the screen. And based on the expression of his face, he seems really, really pissed off.

"Chi Richards is wanted for the brutal murder of the Jenison family, found dead at their home this morning. If you see this young man, please alert the police immediately. Do not approach the suspect yourself."

I stand there like an idiot as more nonsense spills out of the speakers. *What the hell?!*

Jane is equally shocked.

When she recovers, she grabs my shoulders.

"How did they find Willow?" I ask.

Jane shakes her head sadly. "They have harsh interrogation tactics. Was that Stephen in the picture?"

I nod. Now I know for sure that they have Stephen. I'm gonna kill all those jerks. I swear to it. If they touch him, they're dead. Every single one of them!

A picture of Mrs. Jenison appears on the screen, with her head smashed open, her blood pooling on the kitchen floor. I close my eyes. I'm gonna puke. *How can they show this on TV? That's propaganda bullshit!* They really want me dead for a crime I didn't commit, a crime that's obviously theirs.

"It's a set-up," Jane says as she turns to me. "They killed them to frame you."

When she sees the tears in my eyes, she pulls me to her chest. "I am so sorry, honey. I know you loved Willow."

I blink fast and swallow hard on the stupid lump in my throat. My fists clench hard. I want to break something. I blink again, but I can't control the tears. Willow didn't deserve this.

Jane pulls back and cups my cheeks. "We will get through this. We'll find your brother and your parents, I promise. I am so sorry, honey."

She kisses my face as she says it, but I know it's all lies. She can't help me find my parents. Neil hasn't been able to locate them yet, and it's been two months already. He said the detainees lose their identities once they reach the camps. They're differentiated by numbers, which makes them untraceable. We probably won't find my brother, either.

"I can't go to school today," I say, changing the subject. "They'll recognize my face."

"Chi, the pictures were awfully blurry. No one will recognize you from those shots."

My stomach curls when I think about Stephen at the hands of the officers.

"You will hide in plain sight, where they least expect you. You've already started school; it would be suspicious and unwise to stop going. They won't think to look for you there. It's an elite school for the sons of officials, Chi. Only the highest members of our society have access to that school. The only reason why we never put Jordan there was to protect him because of our link to the Underground."

I nod and squeeze her hand when her voice breaks like it does every time she speaks Jordan's name.

"If anyone confronts you about this, deny everything and come home immediately. I will make a plan with Neil in case we have to leave."

I shake my head. "I refuse to shatter your lives like I did my family's."

Neil holds a high position as a computer security specialist. His work for the government is essential to those in the Underground, too. He can't lose that job because of me.

"Chi, your parents love you. They trusted us to take care of you for a reason. Go to school and act as if nothing is the matter."

I think about my classmates. Many of them are pretty shallow. Most of the time, all they care about is having sex and getting drunk. The teachers, though, are a different matter. Hopefully, they won't put two and two together. But Jane is right, if I stop going, they'll definitely notice that something's wrong.

Hide in plain sight.

I hope it works.

✸✸✸

Two Days Later

After class, Lawrence comes and stands in my face. "You know, you look just like that guy on TV."

Shit! Well, that didn't take long.

I laugh with humor I'm not feeling. "Right. I'm a fugitive who butchered his girlfriend and that's why I'm sticking around the area like nothing's going on. I'd be really stupid to do that, don't you think?"

Lawrence stares at me. "Yeah, I don't know. You do look like him."

"Be careful, Lawrence. Don't reveal my secret, or you might be next on my list."

I feign a smirk, but I want to freaking cry. Willow is dead. All her sweet family, dead...because of me.

Lawrence laughs at my joke like a moron, and I clench my teeth as he keeps laughing about Willow's death. "You're right. Only an idiot would stick around after doing something like that," he concurs eventually.

"I know, right?!"

"What are you doing after class?" he asks.

I shrug. I'm going to Jane's house, where I'll stay in my room so I don't have to face reality, because I'm a damn coward.

"We could hang out at my house. Fox is coming. He said he'd bring some pot."

I wrinkle my nose. I cannot stand William Fox. The little I've seen of him was enough to tell me he's a jackass of the worst kind.

Lawrence taps me on the back. "Come on, man, it'll be cool. His dope is really good."

Comme si j'avais envie d'me droguer avec une bande de losers. As if I feel like doing drugs with a bunch of losers.

"I'll pass, thanks."

"Meeting a girl?" he asks.

"Nah. Doing homework."

Lawrence makes a face. "You're passing on dope for homework? You got a screw loose or something?"

"Something like that. We've already established I'm a psychopathic killer, remember?"

Lawrence laughs. I grit my teeth.

"You're never going to be popular around here if you don't join in on all the fun stuff, man."

I shrug and walk away without looking back, but I hear him laughing at me. I grind my teeth again.

"Don't be like that, man. Come on. It'll be fun," he calls out to me again.

I flip him off over my shoulder as I open the door to the bathroom. Lawrence laughs again as the door closes behind me and I find a stall. I lean against the wall. I hate this place. I hate my life.

Willow's face appears in front of my eyes—her sweet smile like a sword through my heart. I never should have been born. A sweet girl died because I exist. I fucking hate myself.

✸✸✸

The next day isn't any better.

"Ever heard of The Joy of Life?" Fox asks.

Please, get him out of my face. I'm in a worse mood today than I was yesterday. And now Fox is trying to make small talk, as if my day didn't stink enough as it is.

I shrug at his question.

"Been there a few times," he adds. "There's that one girl there, Lillian. Damn, she's a good lay."

Bile rises into my mouth. *Is he talking about a prostitute at some brothel?*

I try to hide my disgust and Lawrence asks, "Was she your first?"

Fox frowns. "No, that was Joy. I already told you that."

"Who's Joy?" I ask.

"Just a girl I bang on a weekly basis," William replies with a smirk.

"Who's Lillian, then?" I ask.

"Same thing." William winks, and my insides knot together with bile rising in my throat.

"Well, I have to pay for Lillian," he adds. "But she's much better at it than Joy. Totally worth every single penny."

He grins at me, and Lawrence asks, "Do they do group rates? If you recommend me?"

I don't know why he's asking. I've already figured out that he's gay. He's implied more than once that he'd like to get in my pants. He tried to be subtle about it. Lucky for him, I'm not one of those homophobes walking the halls of our school. I won't tell on him. I don't care who he sees or why as long as he gets off my case. Even if I were gay, I wouldn't have sex with some misogynistic prick like him.

Fox is too dumb to realize Lawrence is putting on a show and that he actually likes guys.

"You mean a discount?" Fox asks.

"Yeah, if I go there because you told me about the place, do you get a discount for your recommendation? Or can I get a discount?"

Does he realize he's talking about girls? Actual human beings. And not some merchandise to be purchased at the store.

"I can ask," Fox replies.

I want to face-palm myself and bang my head against the wall until it bleeds or until I get a concussion and pass out. Really, anything so I don't have to listen to their moronic discussion.

"How about you, Wilcox? I'm ready to lend Lillian to you for an afternoon."

As if she belongs to you! Connard! I take a deep breath and try to repress the deep urge I have to break his face.

I'd never heard about those brothels until I came to this school. William bragged about how he's not supposed to go there because his dad hates it when he uses his last name to get favors. But apparently, these prostitutes are part of the many "perks" upper-class men get when they have the right status. Most of the population doesn't know about them. Those girls get picked up from the streets after being cast out by their families, and then morons like Fox get to use them at will. I can't stand the mere thought of it, let alone participating in it.

***

Two Years Later
Chi - Nineteen Years Old

"I still haven't found Stephen's location, but I know where my parents are," I tell Taylor during one of our weekly meetings.

He leans against the desk of his high-class study and squints his eyes. "How did you find out?"

"Tina told me a few days ago."

Bryan, Chase, and Kayla all look at me, and Taylor narrows his eyes.

"Okay..." he says.

"They're in Camp 19."

Bryan throws me a look.

"May I talk to you for a second?" he asks.

When Tina told me my parents are being held in Camp 19, she claimed she didn't know where Stephen was. So I asked Bryan to see if Stephen might be in that camp as well. He told me it'd be hard to find out, but he'd look into it.

I follow him out into the hall.

"So?" I ask. "Did you find him?"

Bryan clears his throat. "Yeah."

"And?"

Bryan averts his eyes. "Are you sure you want to hear this?"

I nod. "Yes, or I wouldn't ask. I've been looking for him for two years. Is he okay?"

Bryan looks me straight in the eyes. "He works for the authorities."

A lump settles in my throat.

"What? How?"

"As an officer."

My throat closes upon itself. I'm going to throw up.

"How? Why?" I ask, though of course Bryan wouldn't know the answer.

He doesn't know Stephen like I do.

My brother has finally managed to push his hatred for our family to its limit. He's working for the very people my parents hate.

He's working for the very people who have persecuted me my whole life, for those who coerced me to hide since I was born, then forced us to flee when they found out about me. My own brother is working for those who would kill me on sight if they ever caught me alive.

I knew our relationship had degraded over the years. But I thought he still felt love for me, somehow. I'd never realized he hated me that much.

This is a sword to my guts. I can hardly breathe. My own brother hates me so much he's working for those who want me dead.

My own twin brother wants me dead.

For two years, I have felt pain, as if he were calling for help. But it was just his hatred for me running through his veins, calling out for my destruction.

I guess it makes sense. He hasn't had a kind word for me in years. He's obviously hated me since childhood. I just didn't want to accept the truth.

I grit my teeth and face Bryan, who's looking at me with pity.

"I gotta go."

I can't face anyone right now.

In my peripheral vision, I see Chase glance at me from the door of the study. I pretend I don't see him and keep on walking until I'm out of Taylor's house. Jane isn't supposed to pick me up for another two hours. I'll take the train. I can't stay here. I need to think. I need to process this, even though I doubt I'll ever accept this new reality.

244

Holding Ground

Willow

A Short Story 2

To be safe is
to avoid life, apparently.

Alice Rachel

Willow: A Short Story 2

Willow - Seven Years Old

"I'll see you at four, Sis," Lila says as she picks up her backpack.

"Have a nice day, Lila."

She smiles and I'm still waving goodbye when Mommy walks into the foyer. Lila closes the door and I wrap my arms around Mommy's tummy really tight.

"I'm going out to look for some mushrooms," she says. "Are you coming?"

She always asks me if I want to come along like I have a choice, but I'm not allowed to stay home alone. I nod a few times before I put on my shoes. Then she takes my hand and leads me out.

I always have trouble keeping up with her when we walk through the woods. And sometimes, Mommy doesn't take the normal path and my hand slips out of her grasp. But I try not to lose her, and every so often she casts glances at me.

"You're okay, sweetie? Do I need to carry you?" she asks.

"No, Mommy, I'm okay."

I scurry after her, but a bunny catches my attention. I stop in my tracks to look at it. Mommy taught me not to move when I see a wild animal, so I stay there and watch the bunny. His little nose moves as he sits still. He's so cute. I wonder if the bunny would let me pet him. He scratches the leaves all around with his paws, and when I look up, Mommy is gone. I gasp, which scares the bunny away.

"Mommy? Mommy?" I call, running through the woods.

"Willow, over here."

I follow her voice. My foot catches on a root when I run to her, and I fall face down on the ground. My knees hit a rock and I let out a little yelp. Mommy appears among the trees, rushing toward me.

"Willow, aw, sweetie." She comes to me and crouches by my side.

I blink fast because I don't like crying in front of Mommy. It makes her really sad when I cry, and I don't like it when my Mommy is sad. She strokes my hair away from my face and kisses my forehead.

"Did you get a booboo?" she asks sweetly.

I nod and one tear rolls down my face before Mommy kisses my cheek. "That's my big girl, yes?"

I nod and look into her deep blue eyes.

"I didn't even cry," I say, puffing my chest as I rise to my feet. "See!"

She smiles at me. "We'll disinfect the booboo at home. You're going to be okay long enough to help me find the mushrooms?"

"Yes, Mommy, I'm fine."

250

I look at my leg and see a bit of blood. The booboo itches, but I smile at Mommy when she ruffles my hair and winks at me before taking my hand.

"You stay right by my side this time, okay?"

I do as she says and we enter a clearing in the woods.

"There was a bunny, Mommy. He was so cute. That's why I stayed behind."

"You can't wander away, Willow. The woods are dangerous. What if you get lost?"

"I know, Mommy. But the bunny was really cute."

Mommy laughs and bends down to leave her basket on the ground and pull me up into her arms.

"Can I have a pet bunny, Mommy?" I ask.

"Wild animals are happier outside, sweetie. We've already discussed that."

"When we've found the mushrooms, will we go to the stream? I saw a frog there the other day. Can I have that frog as a pet?"

Mommy shakes her head while rubbing her nose against mine. It always tickles when she does that, and I giggle. Then she puts me back down and we start looking for mushrooms. I try really hard to find as many as possible, but I only find a couple. Mommy already has at least ten of them. I stand there and look at her. *How did she find so many?*

"How did you find all the mushrooms, Mommy?"

She looks at the ones I'm holding. "Those are not good, Willow. Drop them."

"How do you know?"

"See, these ones are morels," she explains while showing me the strange mushrooms she's already put in the basket. "Look! They have black or brown uppers with little holes in them. The ones you picked up are white. They're called amanitas and they're poisonous."

I drop the mushrooms when Mommy says "poisonous." Poisonous means I'm going to be really sick and die if I eat the mushrooms. Mommy told me that when I was really little.

She takes out a small bottle of liquid that she sprays on my hands before she wipes my palms with a napkin that she has pulled out of her pocket.

"Stay by my side. I don't want you to pick up bad mushrooms again. And as soon as we get home, you will wash your hands."

We stay in the clearing for a while, and by the time we leave, the bottom of Mommy's basket is full. She takes the few mushrooms I found and thanks me.

"Let's go home. I'll make an omelet with these and the eggs we're going to pick up now."

"Do you think Gina is still sick?" I ask.

Gina is my favorite hen. She's had a bad case of fowl pox. We've had to keep her away from our other chickens because Mommy said the disease is contagious. I didn't know what contagious meant, but Mommy said it means the other hens will get sick if they get close to Gina. I cried when Mommy said it, but she gave me a big hug and told me it would all be fine. She explained that Gina got the disease from a mosquito, but that she should be fine soon.

It's been a week though, and Gina was still sick yesterday.

"She's recovering, sweetie. Don't worry about Gina. She will be fine, I promise."

"So we won't eat her, right?" I ask. "You promise?"

Mommy gives me a tiny smile. "No, sweetie, we won't eat Gina."

I threw a fit last week because Daddy killed one of our chickens for dinner. I cried and cried and screamed even, and Daddy got upset at me because he said I was being difficult. But I don't want to eat my pets I told him, or any other animals because they are my only friends besides Lila. Daddy looked at me sadly and nodded his head, but he said I still had to eat meat. I refused to leave my room when it was time for dinner because I'm not okay with watching my family eat one of my friends. I sulked for a week and I'm still mad at Daddy.

"You promise?" I ask Mommy again.

"Yes, I promise we won't eat Gina."

Mommy grabs my hand and we walk side by side even though I slow her down because I can't keep up with her long legs. Because I'm so short, I don't need to duck under the branches, but I can't wait to grow taller so I can climb trees like Lila does. Lila is much bigger than me. She's nine already and very tall. One day, I will be big like her. And then I can climb trees and go to school. Just like her.

"Mommy?"

"Yes?"

"When will I go to school like Lila?" I ask. "She's only two years older than me. I know she was going to my school when she was seven. I remember."

Mommy gives me a sad glance, and she looks away before she lets out a long sigh.

"We'll talk about it when we get home, Willow. Okay?"

Mommy always says that, but she never gives me the answers I want. Sometimes I forget I asked. But I'm going to try and remember this time because I really want to go to school.

✶✶✶

When we get home, Mommy leaves the mushrooms on the kitchen counter and opens the fridge.

"Mommy, can I go to school soon?" I ask again. "Lila told me she's learning math, and she knows how to read. When will I learn how to read, Mommy?"

Mommy's shoulders sag as she closes the fridge. Then she looks at me sadly again. She tilts her chin toward the living room and asks me to follow her. I run in front of her and jump on the couch even though I'm not allowed.

"Willow, don't jump on the couch."

I giggle and fall on my behind before settling down with a cushion on my lap. Mommy comes to sit next to me and grabs one of my hands. "Remember when I said we couldn't go to the city or leave the forest?"

I nod. I'm not allowed to go shopping. Daddy goes with Lila while Mommy stays here with me. I've never seen a city before, but Lila showed me a book once that was called *Eboracum City, or the New State Capital.* It had pretty pictures of shops with wide windows and plenty of people walking around. I asked Mommy when I could go to that Eboracum City place, but she told me we couldn't go. She never said why, though. I asked every day for a week after that, but then Mommy got a bit upset so I stopped asking.

"You know how I said that people couldn't find out about you, sweetie? How there are mean people out there who would hurt you if they knew about you?"

I nod and swallow hard. My heart hurts because now it's beating fast. I don't like the mean people who want to hurt me. And I don't like it when Mommy talks about them, either. She already told me those people would do bad things to me if they found me, but she didn't tell me why. She kept saying "Unwanted," but I don't understand that word and she didn't explain when I asked. But I know I have to hide from the mean people. That's why Mommy and Daddy are keeping me here, in the forest. But I don't understand why Lila doesn't need to hide. She gets to go to school and have friends and everything.

Mommy is about to talk about the mean people some more. I can tell and I just want to hide under the cushion. The mean people give me nightmares sometimes. In my nightmares, I run through the forest and they run after me and then they catch me. They look like big scary monsters. I even had a few accidents in my bed during the bad dreams, but Mommy said it was normal to be scared. I don't want to be scared anymore. I want to go to school, and I want to go to that Eboracum City place, too.

"I will teach you how to read and how to write, Willow. I will also teach you some math. We can use Lila's old school books."

I sigh. I never get anything new. Everything I own used to belong to Lila: her clothes, her shoes, her toys. Mommy said they don't have enough money to buy me new things, but everything Lila gets is new while everything I own is used and ugly. I pout when Mommy says I won't get new school books and we'll use Lila's instead.

"But I want to go to school," I insist.

Mommy taps her lap and I move to sit on it. She wraps her arms around my tummy and kisses my temple.

"Sweetie, you know Mommy and Daddy love you very much, right?"

I nod. "And Lila too," I say.

"Yes, and Lila too," Mommy replies. "Did I ever tell you the story of your birth, sweetie?"

I shake my head.

"You see, Mommy and Daddy belong to the middle class. That means we were only allowed to have one child. Before you were born, Mommy had a surgery."

"What's sugary?"

"Surgery, sweetie. It means some doctors operated on me so I wouldn't have another baby. But Daddy and Mommy

256

really wanted another child and we were really sad. Thankfully, the surgery didn't work, and then a miracle happened and that miracle was you."

I turn around to look at Mommy.

"You are our miracle and our secret, sweetie. When I was pregnant with you, we moved here so I could give birth at home and hide you. Daddy got a new job. We loved you so much even when you were in my tummy, and we are so happy to have you. Daddy cried when I told him I was pregnant with you." Mommy sighs. "But people from the middle class are only allowed to have one child."

I looked at Mommy again. "What does it mean?"

"It means that some mean people think you never should have been born, sweetie. But Mommy and Daddy didn't care about those people's opinions because we wanted you so much."

I blink. I think I understand. "What would the bad people do to me if they found me?"

"Don't worry about that, sweetie. Mommy and Daddy are here to protect you, always. But you can't go places where those bad people are. Like the city, for example. We need you to be safe."

I nod, but say nothing.

"I will teach you how to read and write and everything else Lila is learning that you want to know. But I also want to teach you how to survive in the wild. I want you to know how to live in the forest without relying on any resources besides what nature has to offer you."

She strokes my hair.

"Lila said she has friends. Will I be able to make friends someday, too?"

Mommy's face turns really sad. "Lila is your friend."

"It's not the same. She told me her best friend is named Melinda."

Mommy sighs and changes the subject. "Daddy said he'd bring you a surprise today. Are you excited?"

"Is it the paint I asked for?" I say, rising to my feet and jumping up and down.

"Maybe. We knew you wanted something of your own."

I make a little dance and twirl around. *Yes! Finally something just for me!*

"Can I take it outside?" I shout. "And then I can paint the frog I saw by the stream."

"If you promise not to lose anything. Paint is expensive."

I nod ten times or twenty, and Mommy pulls me into a tight hug. "I love you, my sweetie."

"I love you too, Mommy."

✱✱✱

Willow, Nine Years Old

"Is it bad if the neighbors see me?" I ask as Mom and I walk by the house where new people moved in a few months ago. Mom said the people are really shy, and no one opened the door when she went to greet them.

"They're obviously not home right now. But it's best if you don't come around here alone. I need to meet them first and see what kind of people they are."

Something crashes inside the house as if someone has broken some plates or glass, and I hear a little boy's voice yelling, "I hate you. I hate you. I HATE YOU!"

"Come back here this instant and clean up the mess you've made!" a woman screams. "Wait till Daddy comes home and hears about this."

"Clean it up yourself." A loud bang echoes through the house like a door being slammed.

"Come back here and apologize, you hear me?!"

"No. I hate you!"

Mommy covers my ears as she pushes me forward quickly, but I can still hear the bad words the little boy keeps yelling at his Mommy.

"I thought you said there was nobody home," I say.

"I guess I was wrong. It might be best to avoid this place in the future, sweetie. I don't like the sound of what's going on in that house."

I nod, and Mommy and I move into the forest.

"Daddy's coming back at five today," she says. "He'll take you hunting."

I let out a whimper before I can stop myself. Mommy turns her head to me. She knows I hate it when Daddy hurts the animals.

"Remember what I said before, Willow."

"Yes, I need to learn how to feed myself in the wild," I reply.

"Exactly."

"I'm never going to kill an animal, though," I protest and cross my arms as I crease my face into a frown.

Mommy looks at me. "Being difficult doesn't become you, Willow."

I look away and pout.

"Sulking now, are you?" she asks, with a tiny lopsided smile.

I don't reply. I don't like hunting and I don't like killing animals. I already said it and said it. If Mom and Dad don't want to listen, fine! But I won't go this time.

"Daddy will be sad if you don't eat his game, sweetie."

I mope some more, with my bottom lip sticking out. Daddy doesn't care if the animals are sad when they die. So I don't care if he's sad, either. He's killing my friends, and I don't like him very much right now. "I don't want to go hunt."

Mommy sighs and pats me on the head. "We'll see."

Yes, you'll see. You'll see that I'm not going!

***

The Next Day

"Are you done writing your paragraph, sweetie?"
"Yes."

"Let me see." Mom grabs my paper and takes my pencil to correct my mistakes. "It's 'if I were you,' sweetie. Not 'if I was you.'"

I look at my mistake over her arm.

"You did well. Let's go outside now. I need some mushrooms to season the meat tonight."

I feel nauseated and Mommy gives me a look. "We're not having that talk again, Willow. I won't back down this time. You're eating your meat tonight."

I huff loudly and stand up. When I reach the front door, I pick up my shoes and put them on. Mommy walks by me. "Lock the door, sweetie."

I do as she says and run after her.

When we find the part of the forest that has the most mushrooms, Mommy points at one of them.

"How about this one?" she asks.

I chuckle. "You're trying to trick me. This one is poisonous."

She winks at me. "Yes, yes, it is."

"Mom, when we get back home, can we get some borage from the garden for the chickens?"

"Good idea."

I'll pick up some of the blue flowers for myself too because I love them. *Yum!*

I return to my task and help Mom find a few mushrooms, but I get distracted by the leaves. They make crunchy noises under my feet when I walk. I giggle and start jumping around. *Crunch, crunch, crunch!*

"Willow, stay close."

"Yes, Mommy."

I keep on jumping until a close-by noise stops me. I look up, but don't see anything. But then a boy about my age appears from behind a tree. I blink and wave at him. Mom told me I can't talk to strangers, but I've never seen anyone around here before, and the boy can't be one of the mean people. He doesn't look like one of the monsters Mom has described. A smile appears on his face when I wave, and he waves back. I giggle and go back to Mommy.

✷✷✷

The boy is here every day. He thinks I can't see him, but I know he's there looking at me. I left some fruits behind for him the other day, just to see if he was watching, and the next day the fruits were gone. The boy is really shy though, and I don't want to talk to him either. When I told Mommy about him, I saw the fear in her eyes. She told me not to speak to him. I can't imagine why the boy would hurt me, though. And there's something sad about him, except when he's smiling. I like his smiles.

✷✷✷

Willow - Seventeen Years Old

"**Hello, sweetheart,**" Stephen says, his grin spreading on his face.

I can feel my cheeks burning under his stare. "Hi, Stevie. I brought you something."

"You did?" He cocks an eyebrow playfully and pulls me to him. His hands are warm on my waist even through the fabric of my shirt, and when he bends over to kiss me, I almost drop the basket I'm holding.

He inhales deeply. "You smell so good."

I kiss his cheek and hand him the basket. He stares at it, then at me before he pulls away the towel covering the top.

"Fruit?" he asks, licking his lips as if he's hungry already.

"Mostly apples and pears from our backyard. Technically, I'm not allowed to take them, but I wanted you to have them."

"Why?" he asks, his eyes piercing through my gaze.

Because you look so thin and your brother is an Unwanted, so I'm sure you have to share food with him and that's probably why you're so skinny.

I don't tell him that, though. I don't think he'd like it if I referred to him as skinny.

"Because I love you," I say.

His lips rise on one side. "Yeah?"

"Yes."

He bites his bottom lip. "How much?"

"This much!" I reply as I give him the tightest hug I can.

His smile widens when I let go, and his eyes fill with merriment as he grabs my hand and sits down on the ground, dragging me down with him. I fall in his lap and he bends over to kiss my neck and my cheek, his mouth tickling my skin, making me giggle.

"I love you," he whispers in my ear. "Stay with me forever."

"Always and forever," I reply.

"Willow?"

"Yes, Stevie?"

"Where do you see your future going?" he asks.

"What do you mean?"

He scratches the back of his head when I sit up by his side. "Well, what do you want to do, say ten years from now?"

I think about it for a while. "I want to be an artist."

"You already are an artist," he says.

"No, silly," I reply, tapping his forearm. "A real artist. I want to sell my art and make a living out of it."

Stephen narrows his eyes a bit. "Okay..."

"Dad is helping me grow a clientele. I'm using a fake artist name."

"You are? You never told me that."

I blush. "I don't have much success. Dad has sold a few of my paintings to some upper-class restaurants, but they have very specific tastes."

"Like how?"

"Dad told me that all art is controlled and I can only paint certain things. But I would like to change that. I like art for the sake of art. I don't like painting to make money. I don't like to follow rules when I paint. It's stifling. But Dad said that's the only way I can make myself known."

"Do you believe in using art to make a statement, then?" Stephen asks.

"To make a statement?"

"Yes, what if your art had a double meaning? The surface could mean one thing, but the underlying message would be more profound."

I think about it for a while. "And what message would that be?"

"You're an Unwanted, Willow. You have to hide from the world because of some people you don't even know. You could express that in your art. I mean, don't you ever feel anger?"

"Anger is useless, Stevie. It will only cause me pain."

His lips rise on one side before he pulls me into a kiss.

"And that's why I love you, sweetheart. You are everything this world is not." His smile spreads and his gaze roams my face. "What if you become famous, though? What happens then?"

I look away sadly and push the leaves around with my foot. "Nothing will happen then." I give him a quick glance. "I'm not supposed to be alive. I can't go out there and take credit for my art."

"Who's taking credit for it now?" he asks.

"My dad. He told the restaurants the art was his and the fake artist name, too."

Stephen's jaw clenches. "One day I will take you away from here. You will take credit for your art and have the life you want. I promise."

I look down sadly. "Don't make promises like that, Stephen. It will only hurt me in the end."

He reaches for my chin and pulls my face toward his, pinning his dark eyes on mine. "I *will* take you away from here," he says, his eyes filling with impossible dreams. And when he talks like that, I almost let myself believe him.

I know he's just trying to be nice, but Stephen can't take me anywhere. We can never get married. I'll never get to go to the city. I'll never live off my art or become famous. I'll never be able to have children either because I could never give them a normal life.

Eventually, Stephen will see all that. He'll find someone like him, someone he can live a real life with, and he'll forget all about me. I just enjoy what I have with him now before he takes it all away and breaks my heart. Because I already know that one day, he will realize there is no future for us and he'll leave me behind.

I inhale deeply to push away my welling tears, and Stephen's face turns sullen. "I'm sorry, sweetheart. Did I say something wrong? I love you, and I will take you away from here. You and me together forever. Promise me!"

I look at him. I can't demand that of him. I won't ask him to waste his future on me.

"Promise me!" he insists.

"I promise," I say in a weak voice, and he beams at me again before kissing me and pushing me down against the leaves.

✷✷✷

Willow - Weeks Later

"Willow, is that you?" Mom asks when I come home.

"Yes."

"Where were you?" She enters the hallway. "You weren't in your room. You can't leave like that without telling me. What if something had happened to you? I wouldn't even know where you are."

"I'm sorry, Mom. I'll tell you next time."

"Well, where were you anyway? You weren't at the barn either."

I lick my lower lip. "I was with Stephen."

"Again? Willow, you know how I feel about that," she scolds me, though not harshly. "We've already had that discussion."

"He's safe, Mom. He would never tell anyone about me."

Mom sighs. "That's not the point, sweetie. You're putting him in danger. I already explained all that to you. This won't go anywhere, sweetie."

"So I'm not allowed to be with anyone ever in my life?" I ask.

"I didn't say that."

"Yes, you did! I can't have a normal life or go anywhere or date anyone. Why did you give birth to me, Mom? Why am I here if I can't have a life?"

My heart aches when I see how much my words hurt her.

"You don't mean that, sweetie," she says.

I don't reply, but I do mean it. *If I can't do anything with my life, then why live at all?*

Mom and Dad will die someday. *What will happen to me, then?* I know Stephen will leave me eventually too when he finds someone else he can actually be with. *Is it so bad to have him while he still wants me?*

I don't look at Mom as I run to my room.

"Willow?" she calls after me, and when I don't reply, she comes up the stairs, opens my door, and finds me sprawled face down on the bed, with my head hidden under the pillows.

The bed moves when she sits by my side and strokes my shoulder. "Willow, you know what they would do to Stephen if they found out about the two of you. You're putting him in danger and you're being selfish."

She pulls the pillows away.

"Stephen's brother is an Unwanted," I say, staring at her. "Stephen is already in danger because he's related to Chi. You're lying to me to make my life difficult."

Mom sighs heavily. "I already told you Stephen's mom wants him to have a normal life. She doesn't want you to see Stephen anymore, sweetie. Stephen is her son. I can't allow you to go against her will."

I stare at her. "What about what Stephen and I want? He loves me and I love him."

"I know, sweetie, but he can never have a life with you. Don't you want him to be happy?"

"I make him happy," I say.

"Maybe for now. But how happy will he be when he can't leave these woods because of his attachment to you, sweetie? How happy will he be if he can't have a normal life? It's a huge sacrifice to ask of someone. Your Dad and I, we love you more than life itself. We wanted you, and we can't live without you. But you are our daughter. Stephen, though, is a boy who doesn't understand what such a life entails."

I shake my head. "He already knows. He has lived his whole life with an Unwanted."

"Yes, he did. But don't you think he deserves freedom? That he deserves a different kind of life? Please, think about it."

She pats my shoulder and stands before leaving my room. I drop my head on the pillow and close my eyes. *Is Mom right? Would Stephen be better off without me? Will I only drag him down or keep him from moving forward?*

My heart aches at the thought of leaving him. But deep down, I already know Mom is right. Stephen deserves better than an anchor like me, and someday he will see that too.

***

Willow - Weeks Later

"I don't want to date Chi!"

Mom casts me a sad look, but I can't give up.

"I don't want to hurt Stephen."

"Mrs. Richards won't let Stephen date you anymore, Willow. I already told you that. I can't go against her will. He is her son, after all. She has the right to protect him the same way I want to protect you."

"But why should I date Chi? If I can't be with Stephen, then why should I be with anyone at all? I want to be with him and no one else."

"What will happen when your dad and I pass away, Willow? You need someone. I've explained it to you many times already, sweetie. Give Chi a chance. He's such a sweet boy."

"It will hurt Stephen if I date Chi," I exclaim. "I don't want to hurt Stephen, Mom. I don't want to be with Chi. Please don't make me."

Mom swallows hard on a ball of sorrow.

"Why can't Chi take Stephen's place?" I ask. "Stephen could be the Unwanted and then we could be together."

Mom loses patience then, which is unusual for her. "Do you even realize what you are asking, Willow? You can't ask something like that of Stephen!"

"I know...I just..." My shoulders sag, and Mom pulls me into a hug before kissing my hair.

"Sweetie, I want you to be happy. Please, give Chi a chance. Stephen will move on."

Her words make my heart squeeze with pain. I don't want Stephen to move on. I don't want him to date anyone else. I want him to be with me, always.

Mom cups my face. "I love you, Willow. I only want you to be safe."

I nod, though I don't feel it in my heart. To be safe is to avoid life, apparently.

***

Willow -
The Evening She Is To Run Away With Stephen

I arrive right on time, with a small bag of clothes. My heart aches. Mom and Dad will be so upset when they find out I'm gone. But I'm done listening to them. I'm done hurting the boy I love.

I wait, but Stephen is late. It's not like him. He's always so punctual. That's one of those things I love about him. I can always count on him to be on time. I look around and listen for his footsteps, but I don't hear anything.

After ten more minutes, I grow anxious. Stephen should be here by now. I've been apprehensive since he left yesterday. I've had this strange feeling, and now my doubts are intensifying.

After an hour of waiting, I know something has happened. Stevie would never leave me stranded like this. I'll go to his house. Maybe just walk by. If anyone sees me, I can pretend I was visiting Chi.

I grab my backpack and head that way. His house is not far from here, and soon I see the dark roof. I walk toward the entrance and find the door ajar. My heart is hammering fast, though I can't explain this pain in my chest. Something isn't right here.

I walk up the steps and knock on the door, but no one answers, so I push it open and step inside.

"Hello. Is anybody home?"

No one replies.

"Chi? Stephen? Are you there?"

The house is dark and eerie when I walk into the living room. I spot a stain on the ground, and my legs start shaking. The stain looks like blood. A whole pool of it has dried on the hardwood floor.

"Stephen, are you there?" I shout, panicked as I drop my backpack and run through the ground floor looking for him.

I pass through each room, calling for him frantically. *Where is he? Please, please, please, let Stevie be okay.* I don't see anyone downstairs, so I dash upstairs next. I don't know this place at all. The first room I walk into looks like his parents' bedroom.

272

I head to the next one, which smells like Chi—his distinctive boyish scent mixed with spearmint. I run down the hall next, toward the last room—Stephen's room, I'm sure. I turn the knob, my heart racing so fast I can't breathe. Chi told me the officers had come for him once before. I fear they may have found him again.

I step into the room and turn on the light so I can see better. Stephen isn't here. But I already knew that. My heart deflates all the same as I run out and away from the house until I find my parents in our backyard. Their eyes widen with shock when they see the terror on my face and I tell them we have to find Stephen's family.

✹✹✹

The next day, I visit Stephen's room again. He hasn't returned and now I know for sure that something bad has happened. I tried to run away yesterday to find him, but I didn't go far. Dad was there waiting for me when I reached the road leading out of the forest. He was truly upset and yelled at me for the first time in my life. He told me I wasn't being reasonable, and I yelled back that he and Mom had forced me away from Stephen and now Stephen was gone.

I've hardly talked to anyone since then. If I had run away with Stephen like he asked me to, none of this would have happened. I would have taken care of Stephen out there in the wild and he would be safe.

I look around as I enter his room. It still smells like him, his boyish scent filling my nose, with a light touch of cinnamon. The bed against the wall is tightly made, without a single wrinkle on the covers, and the nightstand table on its side is stacked with perfectly-arranged piles of books. A dresser faces the bed with a stuffed, grayish bunny sitting on top. Just like the rest of Stephen's room, the desk by his dresser is so clean it looks unused, except for a few notebooks in one corner.

I walk to the desk, open a notebook, and find Stephen's beautiful cursive handwriting filling the pages. I fingertip the letters and my heart swells. I open the drawer next and find more books, as well as a journal carefully hidden underneath them. I pull it out and look through the first pages.

I blink at the words and clutch the journal to my chest as I take another look at Stephen's clean, tidy room. There are no posters or decorations on his beige walls. It's wrong that I have the urge to look through his journal again. I try hard not to, but the pull is too strong. I turn the pages and read a few lines. So much anger. So much pain. The date on the page tells me this entry is two years old. Stephen was fifteen when he wrote this.

When I turn more pages quickly to look for a more recent entry, my heart breaks. I stop breathing and the journal falls to the ground as tears fill my eyes. *Oh, Stephen, I never knew! How could they? How could his own parents do this to him?* I tighten my fingers into a fist as more tears roll down my face.

✻✻✻

It's been two months since I last saw Stephen or Chi. Mom said they might have moved away, but that's a blatant lie and she knows it, too. I saw the blood in their living room. I know something bad happened. I don't want to think of the worst. I don't think I could survive it.

I've hardly left my room since I found his diary, and my parents are worried. I cry at night and when I wake up. I stole the bunny from his dresser, but it hardly smells like him anymore. I've read his journal at least ten times already.

Stephen once asked me if I ever felt anger. I didn't understand why he had asked that question back then, but now it all makes sense. The anger I feel is deep and foreign. It's as if my head is about to explode. I can't accept the things his parents did to him. He never told me. He hid his secret so well behind his broad smiles. But now I understand why his smiles never quite hid the sadness in his eyes. And his journal is filled with so much rage, shame, and pain, his words have torn my heart apart and left it in picccs.

I grab the journal to look at the pages I've stained with my tears, when a hard knock resounds from downstairs, followed by shouts and my mom's screams.

I jump out of bed and hurry to open my bedroom door, just in time to see Lila turn around from down the hall where she's standing by the stairs. She makes a shushing sign and shakes her head at me.

"Where is he?" a male voice bellows from downstairs.

"Who?" Mom asks.

"Darling, what's going...?" Father asks. "What are you doing in our house?"

"You're under arrest for sheltering an Unwanted," the man answers.

Lila looks at me with her eyes wide open in terror. She tiptoes her way toward me and pushes me back into my room. Then she closes the door and shoves me in the corner, her body blocking me.

The man's voice rises from downstairs. "Where is Chi Richards?"

"Chi?" I ask in a whisper.

"Shhhhh," Lila scolds me.

She presses her hand against my mouth, her glare warning me to keep quiet.

I can't hear what my parents are saying, but then a shot is fired and my mom shouts my father's name. There's a lot of commotion downstairs as if they are fighting. Another shot shakes the air, and a whimper escapes my throat. Lila's eyes glisten with tears before she pulls me into a hug.

We hear the officers' footsteps coming upstairs, and my heartbeat quickens as I watch Lila's face morph with fear.

"We need to leave," I say through my repressed sobs. "We can climb down the tree."

She nods and we walk on tiptoes. *Are Mom and Dad truly dead?* I cover my mouth with my hand when another sob shakes my body, and Lila gives me a sorrowful glance.

The door flies open.

"There are two of them here," the officer shouts as he steps forward.

"Two? They only have one daughter," someone else replies from the hall.

The man sneers at us wickedly. He points his gun at my sister, and before she can react I shield her body with mine as the officer shoots.

COMMON GROUND: 2017!
FOX'S BROW FURROWED AS HE CLICKED HIS TONGUE. "WOULD JONES BE WILLING TO EXCHANGE INFORMATION FOR HER SAFETY?" "YES, SIR. TAYLOR CARES ABOUT HER MORE THAN LIFE ITSELF."
FOX LOOKED DOWN AT KAYLA. "WELL, WELL, WELL, MISS HAYNES. WHATEVER ARE WE GOING TO DO WITH YOU?"

DANGEROUS GROUND: 2017!

"THE UNDERGROUND IS A MYTH, RAFAEL.
THEY DON'T EXIST."
RAFAEL SENT CHASE AN INCREDULOUS GLANCE.
"THEY DO TOO EXIST. YOU JUST DON'T SEE THEM
BECAUSE THEY ARE UNDERGROUND.
THAT'S THE WHOLE POINT."

CHASE LOOKED AT HIS BROTHER LIKE HE
WAS A PURE IDIOT.
"YOU'RE FREAKING DELUSIONAL IF YOU THINK
ANYONE CAN BYPASS THE LAW
AND FIGHT THE AUTHORITIES."

ABOUT THE AUTHOR

Alice Rachel grew up in France before moving to the Unites States to live with her husband. When she doesn't write, Alice teaches French to students of all ages.

She also spends hours reading books of all kinds (Young Adult, New Adult, Mystery, Horror, Romance, History, Graphic Novels...There probably isn't a genre that she doesn't like). She also enjoys going to the movies, visiting museums with her hubby, taking care of her guinea pigs, and drawing.

Alice loves to interact with her readers (and so do her characters). You can find her on Twitter under @AliceRachelWrit. She also likes to chat through her website at www.alicerachelwrites.com as well as on Instagram, GoodReads, and Facebook. Her drawings can be found on www.society6.com/alicerachel.